# FATHER DREAM

By

Mark Hein

i

Father Dream is a work of fiction. Names, places and incidents are the products of the author's imagination or used fictitiously.

Cover Image is an adaptation of a photograph by Bengt Obergen of sculpture titled *Spirit of Haida Gwaii*, by *Bill Reid,* and licensed under Creative Commons
Cover Design and Art ©2022 by Kathleen Parry
Interior Design and Formatting by Kathleen Parry

To the beloved four, who transformed my life

To the aboriginal poets and singers whose ancient tales tell
us who we are

To Bill Reid, the late master sculptor whose art magically
brought things into focus

And to each person anywhere who struggles to become a
father.

1208 Old Topanga Cyn. Rd.
Topanga, CA 90290

*Chapter 1*

## VANCOUVER AIRPORT

People run and walk, talking and shouting in many tongues — English, Chinese, French, Russian, others I can't guess. Carts clatter across the floor, loudspeakers buzz and drone, children's cries punctuate the air.

But I am silent. I dare not speak. I stand, stunned, facing a mass of green stone.

The stone has been melted and made into bronze, oiled and rubbed to glow like a mountain of jade — deep black-green, under a transparent skin of gold. Its glimmering surfaces leap out, yet I seem to see far into its depths. I feel I can almost fall into it.

The stone's shape is what has struck me into stillness. Giant figures, animal and human, crowd into a canoe. They're like refugees fleeing a war or a plague; yet for all their jostling, forceful movement, they seem also somehow at peace.

The Chief sits in the center atop Frog's back, both facing forward. Scanning the far horizon, Chief's huge eyes hunt for the Family's future. To his left, Mother rows, also staring ahead; to his right, Grandmother wields an oar. Daughter and Son do likewise. Unnoticed, Fox crawls over the Chief's right shoulder. Otter and Rat chase each other beneath the women's legs.

It feels as if they're carrying the world, taking their treasure — life itself — to a place they know of and seek, but have never been.

♦ ♦ ♦

I've been in this airport before.

That time, I was unaware of this spot. As I passed through long customs lines on the main floor, Chief and the Family sat above me; if I had glanced up and back, I would have seen them. But my eyes were looking anxiously forward, for the person who was to meet me.

This time, I'm here alone. On my fiftieth birthday. Not looking for anyone. I've come on an early flight from a city far away, in the desert of the American Southwest. On my way to a job interview. I don't want to go, don't want to take this job — but I fear I may have to.

Standing at the green stone shrine, watching the Family's journey, I feel my chest grow tight.

*I was once a father like you, Chief, leading my family in a small boat ... But I wasn't sure where we were going, and we didn't get there ... Our boat broke apart ... and now ..."*

*It's been a hard year. Very hard.*

*I stayed in Phoenix after the divorce, to be near my children. But ten years later, the paper where I worked was sold, and they cut back staff. So I had to move. Four hundred miles away. Now, with bills piling up, my salary stagnant, I may have to move again, much farther.*

*I remember one Saturday morning, coming to pick the young ones up for the weekend. It was right after Matt, the oldest, had come to live with me. The younger three softly grunted "Hi, Dad" and then were silent in the car. "They're tired," I told myself. But when we got to the apartment, they jumped out noisily into Matt's arms and I knew: They needed me, and Matt, nearby. It meant the difference between having their broken family separated — and having half of it gone.*

*It also meant I could pick up Timmy, the youngest, one or two mornings a week, and spend an hour feeding ducks or tossing a ball with him before taking him to school.*

*The years passed. Matt finished high school and left for the Army. The girls became teenagers ... and soon, only Timmy looked forward to our weekend visits.*

*Then my job disappeared.*

♦ ♦ ♦

"Pardon me ..."

A voice jars me out of my reverie.

"... is this yours?"

I rub my eyes and see an old woman in a shawl. She's holding out an envelope. We look at each other a moment. She seems familiar, but I can't place her.

"Here."

She thrusts it into my hand and turns away.

*I don't think I ...*

Before I can say the words, she steps around the great green statue. I try to follow, but when I reach the other side she is gone. I can see only Grandmother, sitting in her seat, her shoulders wrapped, her oar lifted up.

I look down at the envelope, dazed. I open it and find tickets inside — ferry tickets, with my name on them. They're tickets to a place I've never heard of, "Deer Island."

And a handwritten note: "Happy Birthday, Dad."

*How can this be? I told the kids I was going to Calgary, but ...*

I look again for the woman, but there is only the statue, the Family peering forward intently.

*God, how I wish I could climb in that boat!*

A bell rings, and a voice announces my flight. I pull the airline ticket from my bag to make sure. It's time to go back, to say goodbye to the Family and walk behind them to where the gate is …

But looking ahead, the way they're looking, I see the desk for the inter-island ferry service.

*What if you could make one choice, one choice that would really make a difference …?*

I don't know where that voice comes from, but I hear it clearly. And my heart skips. And I know.

I stuff the airline ticket back in my bag and reach to pat Otter's green stone foot.

"Thank you," I say.

And I walk toward the ferry desk.

◆　◆　◆

"Baaa-aaagh!"

An hour later, the steam whistle roars out, shattering the afternoon calm, making the ferry's deckplates tremble. The ferry is laden with cars, a few trucks and busses, perhaps a hundred people. Its heavy engines catch and push, and it glides slowly into the waters of Horseshoe Bay.

To the starboard, just a few feet away, an abrupt vertical rock bank slides past — fir trees, cedars, and pines rise on its steep face. Far below them, shining up from the dark, clear water, orange starfish and white anemones cling to boulders and pilings.

Slipping out of the harbor's arms, the ferry turns north, toward snow-tipped mountaintops that rise abruptly out of the sea. I've always been entranced, on larger ferries crossing to or from Vancouver Island, by these northern islands. Wrapped in their light mantles of cloud, they seem almost to be guarding the entrance to a mythic world.

Now I'm sailing into the mist, toward them.

Watching the water fold and slip past our hull, I feel again how much I love this wild, island-strewn inland sea. For me, it is a sacred place, the true Northwest Passage, more wonderful and precious than the one the explorers sought.

Gulls dance and call in the air, following us into the channels between the misty isles. Amid this almost unearthly beauty, I feel warm tears slide out of my eyes and down my cheeks

*Chapter 2*

## DEER ISLAND

The ferry's huge mass slams softly against stout wooden pilings, a steel sea monster giving a playful tap to an island that seems not much larger than itself.

A small town's buildings lie scattered across the rocky, grass-patched land between the water and the deep green forest. In the slanting light of late afternoon, the shadows of the nearest houses stretch into the sea.

*Deer Island.*

I feel myself tremble a bit, like the ferry's deck shaking in the thrum of the engines.

The town is tiny: One bad winter storm would surely tear it away. Yet so tempered is the Pacific, in these sheltered waters, that barnacles on the pilings suggest it hasn't risen more than a foot or so above where it's now touching the earth.

Here is a settled peace between sea and land. Here, humans and other animals may sleep safely by the sea's edge. Only an hour away, the ocean's long sweep reaches unbroken from Japan to the western beaches; the surf there pounds all year, its tides rising and falling ten feet or more. In winter, the wild waves toss whole trees of scoured driftwood up onto the shore.

But here, calm. The waters lap gently beneath my feet as I walk off the ferry. Grass grows inches from the narrow beach and its tiny tidepools. Mustard flowers and lupines sprout beside hermit crabs and sea urchins.

"Dad!"

My heart leaps to that voice. I turn — there is Tim, my youngest, smiling and waving in the road.

"Tim! How ... what are you doing here?"

I run, my bag swinging and bumping on my left knee, then I drop it and embrace him. We're both laughing.

"Why didn't you tell me you'd be here?"

His wide smile shadows slightly.

"We wanted to surprise you. And ... we wanted you to start out alone."

Tall now, nearly my height, the youngest of my four children has all but become a man, and he's not yet sixteen.

"Are the others here?"

"No," he says. "Come on. I'll take you to the lodge."

After a warm dinner in the rapidly cooling air, we sit by the fire in our cabin. I'm enjoying the easy, open calm I always feel in his company. No matter what we're doing — eating brunch, cruising a mall, talking in the park while I walk and he skateboards — I feel this complete sense of rest and pleasure with Tim. I've felt it since he was small. It reminds me of the way I've always felt with my brother.

*When I lost my job, had to move, it started what I've been calling — just to myself, when I'm alone — "The Year of the Broken Father."*

*All my life, I knew I'd have children, and I was eager to. But only this year did I discover that in my half-century on earth, being a father is the only thing I've done that I truly care about — the one thing that comes from somewhere deep in the center of me. Oh, I have a degree, I've had a plaque on the door; but there's just one title I'm proud of: "Dad."*

*And now ... I don't hear it much anymore. I'm afraid if I move to Calgary, I may never hear it again.*

Tim has set me to re-packing my things from my clunky leather bag into a backpack frame, to which he has added a bedroll and tarp, a water bottle, and a waterproof survival kit.

"We're going hiking?"

"You'll see," he says, smiling.

As I pack, Tim talks about his first year of high school—the teachers, his first friends. He also shares, with laughter, a couple of recent escapades that I suspect his mother and sisters have not heard about.

I finish the backpack and get up, stretching.

"Did you hear any more about that skateboard company sponsoring you and Cal?" I ask, picking up another log for the fire.

"Maybe we'd better save that for tomorrow," he says. "We have to be on our way at sunrise."

◆  ◆  ◆

First light is brightening the spaces between things, giving edges and weight to their soft night shapes, as I step out of the cabin. After the dew-wet lawn, my feet hit the crunching pebbles and shells of the beach.

"Here she is," Tim says.

He is bent over a small dark shape, wriggling what must be his pack into place. Drawing closer, I see the shape is a two-seated sea kayak.

A large raven stands on the stump where the kayak's line is tied, cleaning one claw.

"Thank you," Tim says softly, as he reaches to release the line; the raven rises a few beats into the air, then settles again.

Tim turns and takes my pack.

"You're still the heavier one," he says, grinning and tapping my stomach. "So you sit in back. Again."

I immediately recall the first time we went in a kayak, on Santa Catalina Island. We paddled out of Avalon's small harbor, around a headland that turned out to be rough volcanic rock when we tried to land on it barefoot.

"Thanks," I say. "Planning to dump me again?"

We laugh, again seeing how he hopped, screeching, among a herd of suddenly awakened red crabs. Meanwhile my weight, and a wave, flipped the kayak over with me in it, thrashing and gulping.

"At least you won't lose a snorkel this time," he says, handing me my paddle. I follow his lead as he drags the kayak into the water.

"The other reason I'm in front," he says, "is that I think I know where we're going."

We manage to keep our feet dry as we launch, then Tim strokes out into the channel and swings the bow to the north.

"Watch for a green buoy, about a mile up," he says.

♦ ♦ ♦

During almost three hours of steady paddling, with a couple of breaks on shore, I have to admit in amazement how badly I misjudged Deer Island's size.

Watching Tim's back in front of me, I also marvel at how quickly his lean frame has filled out, and how well he uses his body. He seems to live in it with such comfort; I recall feeling clumsy and awkward at that age.

*I'm also quietly grateful to see no signs of the drug use that has been a part of Tim's young life.*

*How did this happen? It was so unknown, so utterly absent from the world I grew up in — now it's everywhere.*

*I remember sitting with his mother and about twenty other parents, in an anxious circle in the basement of the treatment center. We listened while our children, one by one, told us about their experiences with drugs. Marijuana, LSD, cocaine, something called "ecstasy" ... a few had even tried heroin.*

*Heroin! I'd heard grizzled addicts on TV talk of "horse" as the worst ride, the one you can't get off alive, the one they all fear. Yet here were these children — my own son not yet shaving — able to get not just weed but cocaine and heroin in the halls at school. Or on the streets of our "safe" suburbs. They carried it in their pockets and purses, next to packs of bubble gum.*

*I'd never even seen pot until I was out of college. How did the world change so drastically, without our knowing?*

*Was it Vietnam, a war that sent home tens of thousands of youths who'd used drugs to get through hell?*

*Was it the prosperity we worked day and night to provide — kids' allowances now counted out in ten-dollar bills instead of quarters, a pair of gym shoes costing more than my first suit, every kid expected to get into college?*

*Was it our fault for sitting silently in front of the "cold blue hearth" that glowed in every home?*

*What happened?*

*What brought us all to this low-ceilinged room, sipping bad coffee, hearing with horror as our children unfolded their hidden lives?*

*Hell, I didn't know how to do the simplest, most*

basic tasks of parenting. Much less teach my kids how to handle a drug dealer, or a bad trip, or an addiction.

The first day my wife and I had a child in our house, I realized that nobody had ever talked to me about how to raise one. It was a conversation no parent or grandparent had ever started; and I didn't know I could ask.

Perhaps I couldn't have. I might have been fobbed off with false encouragement — "You'll know what to do when the time comes" — instead of being taken seriously, answered. That happened a lot in our family. Unless they were about being punished, or about grades, serious talks didn't take place.

I tried so hard to be a better parent, not to repeat the mistakes I'd grown up with. I was open with my kids, explained things to them, let them question. They never heard "Because I said so," or "You're too young to understand." Or just silence. That deadly silence.

Yet now here I was, sitting and listening while Tim and a dozen other youngsters explained the dark, anguished life they'd wandered into, as if they'd followed the Pied Piper into the Underworld.

Tim made it through that six-week program, and has stayed fairly clean since. Though I'm pretty sure he still uses pot; his generation sees it the way we saw cigarettes.

We talked about drugs while he was doing the program, and after, but it hasn't been a theme in our conversations since then. Maybe it should be — but it feels like I'd be harping, expressing mistrust, if I keep bringing it up.

And I remember a sudden feeling as we sat in that basement. A feeling that for most of us, this may be the *first time we've listened — really listened — when our kids talked. As if the drug world that was so unfamiliar to us gave them authority, something they knew about that we didn't. Was this a shift that needed to happen — even if it came at such a terrible price?*

*I don't know.*

Fortunately, we've had no headwind to work against, only a couple of mild currents generated by the islets we pass. Rounding one rocky point, we see a long, curving beach that seems to go on for a mile or more ahead of us. Paralleling it, on our right, is a narrow wooded islet that looks to be as long as the beach.

"There should be a river in the middle," Tim calls back. A breeze hiding behind the headland jumps out and tries to snatch his words away.

In just a few minutes, we see the river — a hefty creek, actually, pushing its modest delta perhaps fifty feet into the bay. The breeze, still blowing, now brings the smell of wood smoke.

"Eagle tree," Tim says, pointing to a white-peeled snag that towers out of the trees beside the river. Eagles likely use it for fishing the river mouth, especially during the salmon runs each fall; they may even nest there.

But as we draw closer, there are no eagles. Only a half-dozen ravens circling the delta, rising and landing and rising again. And a thin line of smoke from just behind the tree line.

"Here we are," Tim says, with a well-earned note of triumph.

"Good work, guide," I say, hoping this day's physical labors are over. Even though we've kept up an easy, undemanding pace, my arms and lower back are feeling the work.

I thank the gods that several months ago, a co-worker convinced me to work out with him once a week at a gym near the newspaper. And I'm glad that soon after, I started walking the mile or so from home to the library and the store, instead of driving. Without the months of exercise, I couldn't have done this.

As we near the river mouth, a man steps out of the woods, onto the beach, waiting to greet us. He stands amid a group of tall, bleached poles of varying heights; they look like the ghosts of trees, two with what appear to be ragged branches still attached.

"My god, Tim," I call forward. "Totem poles!"

I've never seen them before in their proper setting, only in museums. And these are ancient ones, their colors long ago scoured off, their carvings wearing away, the trunks splitting from countless rains and freezes.

"Amazing," he says. "This must be Dan Paul, the man we're supposed to meet. I bet he can explain them. And a whole lot more."

♦ ♦ ♦

Dan Paul helps us drag the kayak up the beach to the tree line; I watch the silver braid of his hair bounce on his stocky back. Although his face bears the weathering of perhaps seventy years, he moves easily, quickly, across the sand.

"These totem poles," he explains, tying the kayak's rope around a small pine, "are different. This isn't an abandoned village. That's where you usually see such old poles. This beach is a ceremonial site. No tribe has ever lived here.

"You'll hear it all during the sweat," he adds, smiling. "This is a special one, a ceremony we do only once each year for the young men of our many tribes. And," he adds, laying his hand on my shoulder, "for a few important guests." He smiles; I smile back, wondering how Tim became connected to Dan and his people.

"We'd better go now," Dan says. "The stones are ready. You made good time."

A sweat lodge. This is a welcome surprise indeed.

*I was sixteen. My first summer driving. I took off in our family's second car and started exploring the back roads of California.*

*I remember wandering inland from Eureka, up a redwood-lined river gorge, and the river suddenly widening into a small, lush landscape like a tiny farming nation. There, on a shop porch, I met old men who calmly told me their community had been there before the Gold Rush. Longer, centuries before the Spanish marched in.*

*This kindled a lifelong fascination, for me, with Native American life. I've been touched, very deeply, by the way the ties between humans and the sacred world around us remain, in their view, unbroken. I've collected books over the years, and a few pieces of art — which the children found wonderful, and then got bored with as they grew older. Even though their mother is half-Native, her dad being from a Plains tribe.*

*One of the spiritual practices I had learned of is a*

*widespread one known as sweat lodge. I had long hoped I could be invited to one. But as a city-dwelling newspaperman, I'd accepted that it would probably never happen.*

*And now here I am.*

I smile to Tim, putting a hand on his shoulder.

"Thanks," I whisper.

He smiles back briefly. Then we step into the light underbrush behind Dan Paul.

♦ ♦ ♦

Outside the lodge, a flat dome of cedar planks still bearded with their shaggy bark, we put down our packs. From his, Tim takes out three packets wrapped in brown paper.

"Food," he says, and hands the largest one to Dan Paul.

Dan nods, lifts the packet to his forehead, then turns and puts it in a deep basket. In it I can see loose potatoes and apples, and a bright bunch of carrots, as well as other packets.

"Tobacco," Tim says, handing the second packet to Dan, who nods and lifts it again, and lays it in a flat basket on a stump beside the first.

Tim opens the third packet and turns toward me.

"It's money," he says, pulling it half-open. I fish out my wallet and add my dull green American bills to his colorful Canadian ones. He closes the wrapping and hands it to Dan, who nods and sets it in the tobacco basket.

"Okay, purification time," Dan says, clapping his hands. At his direction, we take off our shoes and socks, then rinse our hands and faces and feet from a bowl of cold, juniper-scented water.

A wiry man of about forty nudges open the tent-flap door for us. He holds a braid of smoldering dried grass in one hand and a large, black feather in the other. Silently, he waves the smoke over our heads and our whole bodies as we enter.

Inside the lodge, it is already hot. Smells of burning cedar and sweetgrass suffuse the dark room; so does a red glow from the fire pit. Dan Paul takes us to our places then goes to the center beside another elder to officiate. They move fluidly between several languages so we all can follow.

First, there is welcoming, naming the people of the land; then each of us introduces ourselves and our people. Then there is singing, and praying. Then the baskets of gifts are brought forward and blessed. In the fire pit, mounded glowing rocks that have been heating since before dawn make loud hiss and spatter sounds, cracking and steaming each time water is poured on them. With the steam, the sweet-grass incense, and the smoke — and the tobacco smoke that curls up as each of us shares the long, carved pipe — the room fills with a deep haze, moist and aromatic. And it grows steadily hotter.

Among the many sacred figures invoked, most are ancestors whose names I have not heard; others are totem animals I recognize, creatures who have made this land their home since long before the coming of the "two-leggeds," or "younger brother," as their kinds call us. Into the smoky, steamy room are invited Raven and Wolf, Bear and Otter and Frog, Whale and Eagle, Beaver and Salmon. The Tree People are invited, including wise old ones known by individual names who are important to the life of the island.

Sweating, we peel off layers of clothing. After many chants and prayers, we enter a time of quiet, meditating while a sole drum beats softly. By now we are naked, or wearing only animal skins or towels, and I can sense the Older Ones about us in the flickering light.

Then Dan Paul clears his throat, inhales and releases a long sigh.

"Chief Eddie," he says.

A thin old man wearing a beaded deerskin vest, with white hair almost to his waist, stands. The drum stops. Chief Eddie makes Dan Paul look young. One foot on a split cedar log before the fire, he begins to tell a story; others punctuate the drama with drums, sighs, whistles and shouts. Now and then, he pauses to drink from a stout mug-shaped basket that has no handle.

He tells a story from long ago, "before the ghost ships came, with their ghost white sails and ghost white people." Europeans, whose paleness so uncannily echoed the way tribal artists had portrayed their ancestor spirits since time beyond memory.

Chief Eddie tells, with Dan translating, of a time when a long-headed people came from the south, riding on the backs of Horse and her people. He tells of a chief with a daughter named Moon Princess, "as beautiful as the moon." She was asked for by men from islands near and far. Her father, who was known for his wisdom, saw that this could become a terrible conflict. So, he made all the young men enter the sweat lodge and become brothers.

"And now, in this lodge," Chief Eddie says, looking hard at each of us in turn, "we are becoming brothers. We are being bound to each other, just as they were — in the passing of the pipe, in the sharing of smoke and sweat and prayer."

After many tests, Moon Princess finally chose one of the suitors, and all the others swore to honor the union as if it were their own. But late in the night, Leather Pouch, a chief's son from the long-headed people, stole the chief's daughter and carried her to his island, far away.

Thus began the first war the people of this region had ever known. Until now, they had raided one another's villages or fields, or squabbled over fishing grounds, in what had become after centuries of settled life more sport than actual battle. It seldom even required the giving of serious injury.

But now, men in each village set aside their sacred duties in the round of life, left homes and families and villages, and took up hunting weapons and fishing canoes to become warriors.

"This beach," the old man says, "this long, long beach, where no village lived, was the only place big enough for so many ships."

More than two hundred ships, their bows carved with the beaks of birds and the teeth of animals, each carrying as many as twelve men, were beached on the long, curving sand. When they were making ready for the ceremony to dedicate their war, uncertain how to proceed, the one who had been chosen War Chief heard disquieting news from his tribe's medicine chief.

The shaman had been walking in the edge of the

forest, meditating, seeking guidance for this new and unfamiliar enterprise. Suddenly, a deer leapt across his path, a young doe close enough for him to count the fawn spots on her rump as she flashed by his astonished face. Amazed, he followed, keeping the doe in sight, trying not to scare her.

"One moment," the old man says, "she stopped to taste the wind. That same moment, before her breath reached her heart, a giant black she-bear rose up before her and — slash! —with a single stroke, the deer was dead. Here, where this lodge sits. This spot, where a lodge has sat for many years of years."

Again, he looks us in the eyes, one by one.

"Here. This lodge. This spot."

The shaman knew the deer's death was an omen. He told the War Chief he could, to his deep dismay, understand its meaning.

At this, Chief Eddie stops. He sips from his woven mug, but does not continue. We all sit in silence, sweating, pondering.

*I am stunned by the bear's sudden, lethal act. I know, somewhere in my mind, that it's natural — but all through my body I feel terrible, sickened, as if a cruel darkness has been hiding in the heart of the woods, of nature itself ...*

*I also tremble a little ... I feel guilty for being here, as if I'm unknowingly trespassing on a sacred spot ...*

"Time for the river," Dan Paul announces.

He rises, and the men begin to follow him to the door and out of the lodge. Those wearing skins or towels

25

drop them. We walk — shocked by the cool afternoon air — down a short path, made soft by generations of cedar fronds and fir needles, to the river.

One by one, we step in its water — another shock — then turn and walk, in a line, toward the beach. No one is speaking.

*I am walking in a river, one of perhaps forty naked men. But it doesn't seem odd at all.*

*The sweat lodge has worked its magic.*

*The smoke and the heat, the drums and chanting have carried me to a different place, a different mind ... The mind I know as "me" is off somewhere, floating, that always-thinking voice silent ...*

*Instead, I am drifting ... in my body — in it instead of wearing it.*

*Yet because of the bear, I sense a tingle of wariness, even as I drift — is danger near? Should I be watching?*

*I can feel, I can hear, I can almost taste the leaves and stones around me. And the water about my feet seems to be flowing into me, and through me, cooling and relaxing ...*

When he reaches the soft mounds of sand in the delta, Dan Paul squats down in the mixed waters of river and bay. Shivering, and roaring softly, he throws handfuls of water over himself. Each of us does likewise, gasping and yelping at the water's touch; but we still do not talk.

After a few minutes, our bodies have cooled and we rise. I think we will go back to the lodge. But we walk north up the beach, following Dan and Chief Eddie.

Before we've gone two hundred yards, we see a clearing in the woods to our left. Sitting in it, one end jutting out over the sand, is a massive boulder; long and narrow, it has an unusually flat, even surface. As we walk up to it, and spread out around it, it reaches about waist high.

Chief Eddie slaps the stone with two hands. Then he sighs again.

"This is Deer Island," he says. "Their home. They live in abundance here. And Bear is their goddess; she makes it so for them, and she helps them into life and out again."

*Then this horrible thing, this fatal surprise ... was natural? Was right?*

*I feel my body shudder like a curtain in the wind ...*

What the shaman told the War Chief, with tears streaming down his face, was that She-Bear required a death: a young doe, the finest of the herd. The War Chief's daughter.

This was devastating news — not only to the chief but to all who knew his people. His daughter was gifted and beautiful, swift of foot and sure of eye, strong in courage and gentle in compassion. She had learned all the arts of herbs and earths and healing, and could catch and tame fish and birds and animals with her hands, talking their language to them.

The name she had been given, "People Mother," expressed the hope that her gifts would spread in her children, ennobling generations to come.

Now She-Bear was claiming her.

27

*As Chief Eddie tells this, I am shaking, my eyes are weeping.*

*I can't take this in ... it is too much. How could any god ask for my daughter? Take my child?*

*"It happens," a small mind-voice says deep inside somewhere. "You know it happens. Children are taken from life every day ..."*

*But my head keeps rolling slowly from side to side.*

*"No ... No ..."*

For three days, the War Chief resisted.

He asked other medicine men to read the omen. He asked them to look for other omens. He begged his brother chiefs to release him, to strip him of his title, let him go away from this new thing, this war.

"I would rather go home in shame," cries Chief Eddie, his voice torn with the War Chief's anguish, "than tear out my heart, my child."

The other chiefs were divided. Many wanted to quit the war. But more did not.

"On the fourth morning, she was brought here." Chief Eddie leans forward, planting both hands on the flat stone. "This rock. It was her altar."

He looks at each of us, silently, and we look down at the stone. Many of us have tears pouring from our eyes like the shaman's. We are fathers, brothers; we have sisters, daughters.

*I'm having trouble breathing.*

*I don't know why I was brought here .. I feel I can't go on ...*

When she arrived, the young girl pleaded with her father, in words and caresses,

"I was first to call you 'father'," she said, "and you to call me 'child'."

But at last, when she knew she would die, she asked to be alone.

"She walked from here right to the place where the young deer had been slain, where the lodge now sits," Chief Eddie says. "No one had shown her, but she knew. She went straight to it. She sat there for three hours, silent."

And when she arose, People Mother had changed. She had become a willing sacrifice. She explained to her ashen-faced father that her name now had a new meaning, one that no one could have foreseen.

"On this rock," Chief Eddie says, "our 'men' were slain with her and reborn as 'warriors.' Our 'people' were changed into a 'nation.' That was what her death brought us."

He bends down and lifts a soft skin pouch onto the table. Opening it, he draws out a long, tapered piece of sharp-pointed antler. It zigs and zags like a piece of lightning caught in bone; on its thick end, the handle, are delicate carvings. A leather thong loops through a drilled hole.

"This is the knife," he says.

He lifts it over his head, in both hands.

"People Mother drank from the sacred ivy bowl, and it stilled her body's fear of pain. Then she laid here, with no bindings on her hands or feet, for she refused them. Her father held the knife in his trembling hands above her, like this ... and he prayed."

Chief Eddie sings a pair of phrases which he does not translate.

"Whunh!"

The knife strikes swiftly down, then stops — just above the surface of the table. All of us have flinched.

He looks at us a moment, then passes the knife to Dan Paul, who lifts it, holds it a moment, then strikes swiftly down, copying the older man's action. He passes it to the next man, who does the same.


*I am staring at the stone.*

*I cannot think.*

*I hear my heart pounding in my throat, a roaring in my ears.*

*I see my daughters lying on the table, first one and then the other, as the knife passes — Emma, then Carlie, Emma, Carlie ... Their eyes are looking up at me ...*

*I hear a high, loud buzzing ...*

*Suddenly I am stumbling, trying to run, but something — underbrush? — pulls at my ankles ... Then I am free, running free, but heavy-footed, as if in slow motion, through sand ...*


I awaken, lying beside the river.

Tim is kneeling, cold water trickling out of his hand and onto my forehead.

"There. He will be alright now." It's Dan Paul's voice; he stands behind Tim. "You can go."

"Dad, you're okay," Tim says. He helps me sit halfway up, on my elbow. "I have to leave, or it'll be dark before I get back. You can stay here with Dan Paul tonight."

*Tim ... is leaving?*

I try to sit up quickly, and get dizzy; he stops me.

"Just rest," he says. "Don't try to hurry. You're doing fine. Stay with Dan. Matt will be here in the morning."

*Matt? My older son?*

Tim rises, hoist his backpack to one shoulder.

I seem unable to move, my breath is coming heavy and ragged like sighing. Still propped upon one elbow, I watch his beautiful, tall form walk away toward the kayak, which sits ready on the shore.

When he turns and waves, my eyes are cloudy and a sob escapes my chest.

Raven hops down the sand, following the receding kayak, calls twice, then rises up and floats back toward us; just past us, upstream, he lands with a whir of feathers.

*Chapter 3*

## HORSE ISLAND

W e're sailing briskly in open water, with only one island in sight. A light, steady wind strips foam from the plunging waves, blowing it back in loose streamers. The small waves look like a herd of wild, white-maned horses, necks above the water, neighing and diving, their mouths dripping from the long, fast run.

Matthew sits in the stern, holding the tiller; he directs me, as his deckhand, when the sails need adjusting. Earlier, we had a busy time tacking between clustered islands, which kept me hopping, ducking the mainsail as it swung back and forth. Now we've reached a large open channel, and we're running before the wind, the mainsail well filled and a spinnaker arching out over the bow.

This sleek, white-painted boat is called the *Mnemos*, out of Victoria.

Victoria — I love that little city. We used to arrive in its small harbor, the kids scrambling down the gangway to greet their cousins. Often, as we stayed in their cabin, we'd all drive into town to enjoy Victoria's museums and shops, its artists and buskers gathered along the brick-walled quay.

This morning, when Matt pointed out the name on the stern, he laughed.

"Remember when Ali and I had to carry you around downtown?"

"I'll never forget it," I said.

*On one of our Saturday afternoons in town, Matt and my nephew Ali and I have gone on a jaunt around the harbor while everyone else stays to explore a giant second-hand emporium.*

*We stroll along the sidewalk, taking occasional side trips into interesting-looking alleys, and down the walkways that lead to boat landings. One leads to the seaplane terminal, where we watch a plane float in, and then watch another load up and take off.*

*Eventually, we work our way around the harbor, past the Empress Hotel and the Coast Guard Museum and the inter-island ferry terminal, and we're picking our way along the rip-rap at the water's edge, in front of some modern luxury hotels. We're hopping from one boulder to the next, flushing birds and peeking into tidepools.*

*I see the sun's gone closer to the horizon, and turn to suggest that we start back; without really looking, I set my left foot on a rock that doesn't appear wet, but is. My leg flies out, and suddenly I'm landing hard among the ragged boulders, with a half-cry of surprise jarred out of me.*

*Matt and Ali rush over and help me up; trying to rise, I feel some sore spots. I also discover that breathing hurts on my left side.*

*"Your shirt's torn in a couple of places," Matt says.*

*"And there's blood here," Ali adds, touching the spot that hurts when I inhale.*

*"Well," I say, trying for jaunty, "this was a little more than we expected. But I was about to say, 'Why don't we head back?'"*

*"We definitely should," Matt says. "And that's enough of the rocks. We're walking on their lawn, whether they like it or not."*

*With one of my arms around Matt's shoulders, the other around Ali, we head back around the harbor. I'm impressed at how strong the two of them are, and how careful, attentive. Our pace is a good deal slower than the leisurely one we'd been keeping, so it's nearing sunset when we finally reach the second-hand store.*

Boy," I say, "I never want to do that again"

"You broke a couple of ribs, right?"

"Yeah, and they took months to heal. Was that summer your last trip up here?"

"It was," he says. "Next time you guys went, I was at Fort Hood. I think that was the summer they made Uncle Theo principal of the school."

"Right. You'd been in the Army about a year then?"

"Uh-huh. A year in June."

"Another day I'll never forget," I say, "is when you told me you'd decided to enlist, just days before you graduated."

"Yeh, a week or so." He chuckles. "You sat on the arm of the couch, looking like you'd just swallowed a frog!"

We both laugh.

"I was shocked alright. But impressed, too, when you told me how you'd been to all three armed services, one by one, and kind of horse-traded. To see who'd offer you the best chance of flight training."

"And the most college money after," he adds. "I didn't figure I could make flying my career."

What he doesn't say, and I don't mention, is that in six years the Army hasn't yet given him a day of flight training.

Matt's long frame is folded jauntily against the stern rail, in jeans and a green sweatshirt. I look, amazed, at his strong-jawed face that seems to brood at rest, his hooded pale-blue eyes, his close-cropped blond hair. Where did this man, this twenty-six- year-old adult, come from?

*Phoebe and I are standing in the sunroom of our little house. In a bright spring morning, birds call. Talking to us is the social worker who's been working with us for almost a year now. She's going over the rules:*

*This is a trial weekend, and if we agree to be Matthew's foster parents, we will have him in our home for an undetermined time — perhaps only a few months, if his natural parents decide not to sign away their rights. We are not to think about adoption, he is a ward of the county ...*

*But I'm not even half-listening.*

*I'm captivated by this small, slender boy of three,*

*with white-blond hair and blue eyes, who has walked in with her and silently set a large brown paper bag on the floor. Now he is standing straight-backed, not listening either. Watching, waiting.*

*When she stops for a moment, he leans down and unrolls the top of the bag. From it he lifts folded blue pajamas, with red-and-white figures on them; he sets them on the floor. He looks up. I smile.*

*Next, he takes out a small pile of white underwear and sets it down. He looks up again. I nod and smile, but holding my breath. We're being trusted, tested.*

*Then come rolled socks, two small pairs of jeans, two T-shirts.*

*"Very nice, Michael," Phoebe says.*

*"Thank you for showing them to us," I say, kneeling down.*

*He turns back to the bag and lifts out one more thing — a small cloth figure, once white but worn grey, with long ears. This, he does not set down.*

*"Your bunny?" I ask.*

*A barely perceptible nod.*

*"Welcome, Bunny," I say. "Would you like to see your room?"*


*That night, after Matthew and Bunny are tucked in, we lie in bed listening. We talk in soft whispers.*

*"She said this is a trial weekend."*

*But we both know it's not. We're already committed, totally, irrevocably.*

*"She said if we have trouble ..."*

*"And if we don't?"*

*"As long as we want."*

*Something that was torn, broken, when the doctors said we could not have children, is beginning to mend.*

*"Unless one of his parents decides to ..."*

*"And if they do?"*

*A pause.*

*"We move to Canada?"*

*We hold hands, listening.*

Warmed by the morning's hard work and the soft but steady sun, I am leaning against the mast, facing Matt.

"You know," I say, "of all the kids, you're the one who's taught me the most."

"Well," he says, smiling, ducking his head, "I *was* first."

"Yes, there is that. But again and again, you keep showing me that what's inside you is something I can't take for granted — heck, sometimes I can't even guess at it."

He laughs quietly.

"At first, I thought it was because you came to us from a past life that I couldn't know. But then the other kids came along, and I finally got it. Even if we share the same genes, I have to find out from each of you who you are."

"Yeah," Matt says. "And it isn't always easy telling you."

"Ouch," I say. "Like with Rosa?"

"Yep," he says, grinning. "That time, *I* was the one on the couch."

I feel my cheeks grow warm with the memory.

*A year away from graduation, Matt suddenly wants to drop out of night school, where he's been making straight A's, and switch to daytime classes at the school where his girlfriend goes.*

*I'm furious.*

*I moved across town to get him into the night school program, so he could work days at a "real job" — which he'd been begging to do since he was twelve. He's made a success of it, for two years, enjoying his work and his paychecks. And erasing the Ds and Fs from a miserably unhappy first year of high school.*

*Now it's all in jeopardy, because he has his first girlfriend and she's telling him she wants to have his baby — at fifteen!*

*"You cannot go and live with Rosa at her mother's house," I shout.*

*Then I see shock on his face as he falls backward — I've shoved him, pushed him back when he stood up to leave.*

"I lost it that day. I'm sorry."

"Well, I don't know, Dad." He is coiling a length of line around his hand. "To tell the truth, I was actually kind of relieved. Not right then, but soon enough. I knew I wasn't really ready to deal with being a dad, or 'the man of the house.'" He grins. "But I didn't have to say so — I just told them you wouldn't let me."

We laugh again.

"You did move in with them, eventually."

"Yeah, six months later. By then, things were different. The whole baby thing was put off, way into the future. We'd had a scare." He lifts an eyebrow, acknowledging that this is news to me. "And Rosa had taken her first art class, and found what she wanted to do."

"I remember you said you wanted to help her get her last year's credits done in one term."

"And she did."

"With bells on, as I recall. You were both on the honors list. *That* was quite a day."

"Not bad for two kids who were gonna drop out and get pregnant, huh?" He laughs and tosses the coiled line into the air, where it spins free.

"Well, thanks for turning me into a dad. I'll never be able to thank you enough."

I reach out and pat his long leg.


*All at once, People Mother's words ring in my ears: "The first to call me father."*

*This is my first child, the gentle golden boy who loved being in church, who wanted nothing more than to have a little brother or sister ... and who happily shepherded all three of his young siblings through their years together.*

*The thing I've never told him, that we've never spoken of, is the horror I feel at seeing him go to war.*

*Could I have stopped him?*

*Should I have stood against his decision, thrown him down on the couch again?*

*So often, it seems, being a parent demands this agonizing letting-go.*

"I'm glad you finally made it back to this part of the world," I say.

"Me, too." He smiles. "It's every bit as beautiful as I remember."

"Quite a change from Bosnia, huh?"

Matt's brows lift, and he shakes his head.

"No kidding."

He's silent for a while, his eyes looking thousands of miles away.

"You know, it's not a bad place," he says. "Up in the mountains, where we were stationed, it's all farm country — like in Germany, around Munich. The mountains ... they actually look a lot like these islands. They're all green, and they've got these beautiful valleys, and all these little villages. Some of 'em still have cobblestones for streets.

"But God, everything's been blown apart. You can hardly see a building that hasn't been hit by mortar fire. And the mines ... they're everywhere. The fields look like Swiss cheese. When we first came in, there wasn't one mile of road that was operational."

"Lynn's letters," I say, "mentioned that you and your team were assigned to map the mine fields."

"Yeah, we did a lot of that. Friend of mine, Cleve, was walking with the sweeper and stepped on one. We thought he was a goner. But it was meant for a truck or an APV — he was too light to set it off. I didn't go sweeping much myself, 'cause I'm pretty good on the computer. So I was in the truck most of the time."

"Scary work."

"Yeah. And seeing so many kids ... their legs blown off, scooting around on crutches. I'm glad it's over. Two tours is one more than I counted on when they sent us to Europe."

"Hard being away from Lynne and Lily so long?"

"Oh, yeah. Didn't get into drinking. Like I told you when I called, there was a bunch of us who tried to stay pretty much on the wagon."

"Yeah, I remember how hard that was for you guys."

"It was hell. With the snipers firing on us, and then the Serbian artillery — just pure hell. And we were under strict orders: No return fire. Ever. A peacekeeping mission. I was sure we were gonna lose it and start shooting each other."

*My insides wrench at hearing this, although it happened three years ago.*

*I never knew how to tell Matt that it tore at me to see him in uniform, to know his life was in danger every day, that he might come home from work one day having killed somebody. Or might come home in a bag.*

*I never told him I cried at the photo he sent from basic training, looking so proud and innocent. Or how I feared each day for his hard-won sense of himself, under the Army's relentless, deliberate battering.*

*Instead, I bit my lip and waited, reminding myself that he so often seemed to know what he needed better than I could.*

"I was mighty impressed with how you handled that whole situation. Bringing Lynne out there was a really good move — even though they made you pay for all of it yourself."

"Best move I ever made," he smiles broadly. "I told her, 'Honey, soon as I had you here to talk to, Hell got a whole lot easier.' But of course, because it was an active war zone, there was no way she could bring Lily — so she couldn't stay long."

*My granddaughter Lily, born at a base hospital in Germany, now almost two. I've never met her, or held her — only seen her in photos.*

*The image that pops to mind is her bright face, long like her dad's, sticking up out of the bathtub under a crown of soapsuds, her eyes and mouth wide with joy as her dad's arms reach for her.*

Matt points north, across our port bow. "Look there. The twin mountaintops."

I watch the eastern end of the island swing into view, with two bald knobs thrusting up above the tree line. High over one, a large bird dips into sight — a bright flash of white identifies it as an eagle.

"Soon as we clear the island," Matt says, "we head north."

We're in a large, quiet bay surrounded by mountains; mist covers the water. The mountain tops peer above the fog, seeming to hang in the air.

We've taken in the sails, and we're floating along quietly. Matt works the tiller, using brief spurts of power from the softly muttering little outboard, listening to hear water lapping against anything solid.

I'm in the bow, watching.

Suddenly, a huge snag lifts out of the fog, like a totem pole floating on its side, just ahead of us.

"Snag, starboard," I call back — Matt swings the tiller. I hook my feet under the bow's narrow railing, ready to lean out and try to push it away if we get close. But we glide by safely. The high, falling cry of an eagle pierces the mist, sounding like it's almost next to us.

After perhaps twenty minutes, creeping along carefully past more floating logs and a couple of weathered trunks that seem rooted to the bottom, we hear a rhythmic clanking.

"Buoy?" calls Matt.

"I'll keep my eyes peeled."

As we move closer, a dense shape starts to gather ahead of us, low to the water like a barge. *Is it moving?* It's where the clanking seems to be coming from.

The fog thins a moment and we see a wooden dock. The noise comes from a small dinghy moored to it, banging its chain on itself in the gentle lapping of the swells.

Matt cuts the engine, steering us to the dock just ahead of the little rowboat. Again, we hear the eagle's cry. Line in hand, I step onto the grey weathered boards. They're slippery with fog and moss. I try to catch our boat's weight and push against it, while I walk backward to the next piling.

While I'm securing the rope, Matt jumps out and secures the stern. We make sure the bumpers, plastic milk jugs filled with sand, are in place between the dock and the boat's hull. Then we step back aboard for our packs, pull the tarp over it all and step back on the dock.

"I guess this is it," Matt says. "Up ahead, there's supposed to be a cabin."

We walk slowly, balancing along the gently swaying dock; when we step onto the land, we're still barely able to see three or four feet in any direction. We pause for a moment, and I'm about to ask how we should explore this invisible landing when a hooded shape steps into the edge of our vision.

"Hello," says a soft, deep voice. "Welcome to Horse Island. We've been expecting you. The cabin is this way."

The figure turns and walks inland, into the fog; Matt and I move quickly to keep up.

♦ ♦ ♦

Inside the cabin, which is more the size of a modest farmhouse, we sit by the fireplace and drink hot tea from hand-thrown stoneware mugs.

Our guide has revealed, throwing back the hood as we stepped into the doorway, that she is a woman: tall, slender and muscular, perhaps in her early thirties, with dark hair clipped short and striking grey eyes.

After setting the kettle back over the embers, she

takes off her hooded jacket and hangs it, along with ours, by the door. She wears a finely woven turquoise dress, and a dramatic scarf in several shades of blue and yellow. On a chain around her neck hangs a gold emblem, a disc that seems almost to be a sun face, oddly grimacing as the rays curve and coil out from the center.

"You may call me Althea," she says. "Please be comfortable while you are here." She hands us each a blanket; they feel as light as if they are woven of silk, yet they quickly warm our chilled limbs like wool. She smiles to see our reaction.

"It is wool — young goat's wool," she says. "I enjoy gathering and weaving it. Isn't it remarkable how warm it is? My father would wear nothing else."

"Did you make your dress as well?" I ask. She smiles.

"Yes. It's a fiber much like cotton; the plant grows wild in the marshes here."

"And where are your silkworms?" Matt asks, looking at her scarf. She smiles again and laughs softly, her large eyes gleaming.

"This was brought from afar," she admits. "But the dyes are from native plants."

We sit for a moment, letting the tea warm us inside while the goat's wool warms us outside. Then she speaks again.

"The story I will be telling you comes from my father," she says. "In fact, my father's fathers, back many generations. I think you may have heard how the Moon Princess came here long ago? And how a huge war party soon followed her?"

"Yes," I say. "The long boats that sailed from Deer Island ..."

"Those very ships," she says. "They landed here, at this bay, where Horse and her people were living, grazing in the meadows beside the marshes and serving the two-legged people — my father's people — who lived up on the highlands."

"The ones the other tribes call ... longheads?"

"Yes." She smiles. "Though I would not use that name."

"I'm sorry," I say quickly.

"I take no offense," she says, still smiling. "This is not only an old, old story — it is also a long, long one. So I will tell you only a small part of it tonight, and then I will let you rest. Even in this century, with sails and motors, it is a long sailing from Deer Island."

While she is talking, a handsome older woman in layered grey and white shawls enters the cabin and goes silently to the kitchen, where she begins preparing a meal. Matt leans back, resting his feet on the brick hearth; I stretch out, too, sore from the days of rowing and sailing.

Althea leans forward, the fire gleaming off her wide eyes, and begins.

"It is, as you know, a story of anger. Anger and weapons, and men."


Yet curiously, it begins with another father and daughter.

Althea tells of how, soon after the hundred ships landed, a strange illness began to sweep through the giant war party.

"Within two nights, nearly one man in three was ill, and a few lay dying." The next day, just at sunrise, a white canoe appeared; two men were paddling, one holding the feathered staff of a chief. Both were dressed in the same white skins the boat was made of. The man who held the chief's staff wore a mask covering his eyes and nose and brow; it shone gold in the sunlight. They carried no weapons, and no sooner had they alighted than the chief made a most unusual greeting.

"I am Sun Priest," he told the War Chief. "You camped on our island during your journey here. Now, my companion and I have come to be your prisoners."

The stunned War Chief asked for an explanation.

"I am to be a hostage," Sun Chief said, "so you will return my daughter, whom you have carried away unrightfully."

Sun Priest reminded the War Chief that after being given food, water and shelter, the men in the longboats had failed to make a thank offering. Instead, they returned insults and blows — even death — for hospitality. He reminded him how the rampaging warriors had taken Sun Chief's own daughter and her maidservant into their canoes, claiming she was a battle prize.

"But has there ever been a battle between us?" he asked.

The War Chief was silent.


At this moment, the older woman brings us each a bowl of stew.

"Thank you, mother," Althea says, smiling and touching her on the arm. "Please join us." The older woman returns with another bowl and sits in the circle with us as Althea continues.

47

The War Chief was deeply ashamed, and in his shame he grew angry. He could not argue with this just charge, nor with Sun Priest's peaceful way of making it. He told Sun Chief he would need a night for consultations and prayers. He then sent his prisoner guests to their tent, and at once convened a council of advice.

"Must I bear this shame?" he asked. "Is there nothing we can do? The Sun Chief *and* his daughter are both now our prisoners."

His shaman was the first to answer.

"Look about you," he said. "Our men are sick, dying. We are helpless before this plague. If this is the offense we have given, we must thank the gods for showing us the way to remove it."

The next to speak was a chief's son from the southern islands, a young man called Orca Smiling, known for his intrepid raids and clever thefts. He was named for his thin-lipped grin, which could seem to laugh and threaten at the same time, like the smile of a black-and-white killer whale.

Orca Smiling had been a leader among those who drove the islanders back by force. He had also led the band who abducted the chief's daughter.

Yet now he said to the War Chief, "You were ill-advised to do this. And a wise leader must accept the blame."

The War Chief was already afire with shame and rage, having seen as soon as the shaman spoke that he had no choice. But now his heart grew calm like a banked fire, because his anger had found a target. With narrowed eyes, he gazed at Orca Smiling.

"*Now* you are wise," he said. "Now you advise me to accept dishonor — while you keep prizes."

Orca Smiling, stung, started to speak, but the War Chief held up his hand.

"I will be guided by you," he told his council. "And you, Orca Smiling, you will take Sun Chief's manservant from me, and give me his daughter's maid, whom you took."

The War Chief then pulled his feathered spear from the ground, saying, "This council is finished. Let us go make prayers for a quick end to the great sickness."

The next morning, the War Chief told Sun Priest he and his daughter were free to return home at once, but they must leave their two servants behind. After a brief ceremony of peace, Sun Priest and his daughter departed.

"That afternoon," Althea says, "the War Chief and Orca Smiling exchanged their prisoners, neither one of them speaking to the other. The next morning, to show his contempt, Orca Smiling freed Sun Chief's companion and gave him a canoe to return home. When the War Chief heard of this, he sent the maidservant home as well.

"The next day, as the sun was rising, the mists cleared; and hour by hour, the illness seemed to dry up in the warmth. By nightfall, none were left ill; of the hundreds who had been stricken, fewer than a dozen had died. But healing the plague — and the offense that caused it — had left a deep, bitter wound between the War Chief and Orca Smiling, one that would cost many lives."

Althea stops, looking intently at me, then at Matt. Then she smiles, and rises. We rise, a bit slowly, stretching.

"Thank you," Matt says, nodding to both women,

49

and I echo his thanks.

"You will sleep well," Althea says. "I will show you where you are to rest."

The next day's sunlight shows us that we're on the seaward edge of a wide estuary, dotted with small green islets, some too tiny for even one horse to stand on. The dock and farmhouse sit on the largest islet, part of a chain that buffers the meandering, reed-fringed marsh from the gentle sea.

Horses graze on almost every bit of land, and there are ducks, coots, herons and other waterbirds everywhere.

Inland, to the east, the reeds grow thicker and the water becomes murkier (except in the river's main channel), until you can hardly tell earth from water. Farther inland is solid ground, perhaps a half-mile wide. Then an abrupt bluff, with stands of large trees at its foot, curves around from far in the south to a headland a mile or so north of us.

We are following Althea and the older woman across a small footbridge.

"As you can see, this is a wonderful home for Horse and her people," Althea says. "Of course, when word came that a great war party was heading this way, my father's people hastened to lead the horses away from here, to valleys in the hills east of their city."

In less than an hour, we have climbed up the bluff and are walking north across a wide, open plateau. To our left, we can see the headland. A finger of the mainland, it reaches out toward what looks to be a huge island. In the narrow strait between them begins a large bay, opening northward as far as the eye can see. The tips of the farthest mountains are just visible across the water, hanging like ghosts along the north horizon.

"Actually," Althea says, nodding toward the huge island, "that's mainland, too. The bay is almost an inland sea, more than forty miles of open water, fed by three rivers."

"Rich fishing grounds," Matt says.

"Very rich. That, and trade, built the city of my father's people."

She sweeps her hand toward the bare, grassy meadow where we stand. Looking down, I suddenly realize that this is not a ridge we are on, rocks peeking out at its crest, but the remains of a wall.

"More than two thousand people lived here," she says. "This, where we stand, was a granary. Stone was reserved for storehouses, to protect against mice and other vermin. Everything else was built of wood — it is so abundant and easy to gather."

Matt and I see an ancient city come to life around our feet as she tells how a nomadic people arrived here with their horses, settled, learned, and became sailors and fishers of the rivers and the sea. She tells how, using their partnership with Horse, they wove a web of contact and trade among peoples who before had barely known of one another's existence.

"And here at the center of the web they sat, making a culture that grew more complex year by year, more cosmopolitan than any that had been known in this part of the world."

She looks down at the ground, and then out, over the water.

"Their villages grew into a city, called Many Smokes, because fires were always burning here — home hearths and baking ovens, smiths' fires and potters' ovens, ceremonial lodges and woodworkers' shops."

"A blessed and happy people," the older woman says, speaking for the first time. "Until Leather Pouch made his fateful journey. He left in honor, to seek a wife. He returned bearing a woman named for the moon, but brought with her darkness. No one knew it, but the sun was about to set here, forever."

We walk to a small stand of trees, and sit in the late morning shade. Althea begins to recount the long tale of the war — the single combats, the boasts of warriors thrilled with their prowess at this new art, the joy of victory and prize-taking, the shock as they watched friends mutilated and slain, the grief as they buried brothers who would never see home or family again.

She tells of massed battles, the shouting and din filling the air, shaking the earth. She tells of silent times, waiting and brooding, the besieged citizens doling out their dwindling supplies as the long war dragged on, the attackers having to forage farther and farther for food.

She tells of the War Chief's struggle to keep unity among his men, as injuries and deaths and hunger hammered at their resolve, making them ache to be home. She tells of Orca Smiling's decision, after a battle in which his dear cousin was slain, to quit the war and take his remaining men home in their boats. And of how the War Chief, angered, let him go, only to see his men routed the next day, nearly a hundred slain, their bodies left to rot in the field.

She tells how the War Chief then had to send his shaman in secret to plead with Orca Smiling, begging him to return.

The sun has passed over us and shadows march silently eastward when the old woman opens a sack and unpacks a meal. But Althea's bloody tale has killed my appetite; I get up and walk away, to be alone.

I find a rock at the roots of a lone tree, and sit in its shade. I look back at the small grove where they sit, and at the city's remains beyond, and at the splendor of the land and water and sky beyond that.

The three of them are eating and talking so easily, on the very soil where so many struggled and died — I wonder what they know, what they understand, that I do not.

*I'm sitting on a boulder, high on a brown mountain. I've dropped Matt off at work.*

*"The Army," I say out loud to the city that lies spread below me, and the desert beyond. "The Army!"*

*I toss a small rock, and hear it clattering down the mountainside. I laugh short.*

*"Now, his grandfather would have said ..."*

*I remember standing in a small airport in Oregon, visiting my parents for spring vacation. While I hugged my mother, suitcase at my feet, my father didn't greet me, just waited across the lobby by the door. He'd never done that before.*

*But this time I was wearing my hair down to my shoulders, a flowered shirt, bell-bottoms — the uniform of a hippie. And back at school, I was volunteering as a draft counselor, helping young men stay out of the Vietnam War.*

*He didn't want to be seen with me. Wanted me to know — to feel — how much he disapproved of who I was, what I was doing.*

*Suddenly, on the mountain, in the blazing light of a desert day, I feel a hand on my shoulder. And I hear my father's voice:*

*"Matt has chosen a world as different from yours as night from day."*

*"A world made of violence," I say out loud. "Made for killing."*

*"A world made of anger, true," my father's ghost says patiently. "But anger under control. All day, people shout orders at each other; they even shout their obedience — 'Yes, sir!' And they learn to use deadly force, in mortal conflicts... Yet they don't harm each other."*

*"So?" Another pebble clatters down the slope.*

*"So do you think you know what part anger plays in Matt's life?"*

*"Anger," I say.*

*I remember driving Matt home from his first day at work, his job new and exciting. As soon as he was in the car, he was telling me his duties, what he did, what he learned.*

*By the time we were home and eating a quick dinner before his classes began, his news report ended with an unexpected coda.*

*"But you know what pissed me off?" And he told of a co-worker who wasn't doing his work, wasn't taking the training seriously.*

*To my surprise, that became a regular part of his daily descriptions, almost a ritual. Each day, it seems, something irritated him. At times, it led to confrontations.*

*I tried to mention this pattern one evening; he frowned, then shrugged it off. But a week or two later, on the way to work, he brought it up.*

*"I'm really not an angry guy, Dad" he said. "I don't get into fights, or even arguments. But I do think a lot about what's going on around me. I think about how things are supposed to be, and why they're not."*

*"Well,' I said, "you do learn fast. You have an unusual ability to get a detailed sense of the system — how it works, what everybody's supposed to be doing, and why. That's a real asset."*

*"Yeah," he laughed, "but getting pissed off isn't, is it?"*

*A few days later, Matt told me he wanted to spend the next three weekends at a program his school counselor had told him about, a workshop for anger management.*

*On a dusty green cactus pad near my boulder, a small orange spider is picking its way among the thorns.*

*"Anger," I say again. Another pebble clatters down the hillside.*

Suddenly, a soft hissing sound explodes near me; I leap up, in a reflex, turning to see what it is — a silver head flies past my foot — there's a coiled, silvery body beside the rock — I'm jumping down, hard, behind the head — someone is shouting — I still hear hissing and feel my heel slamming down sharp, hard, again and again …

A hand grabs my shoulder and I am backing up, trembling, seeing the body lying, half uncoiled, twitching, in torn-up dirt beside the rock.

"Nice work, Dad," Matt says.

"Were you bitten?" Althea asks; she has run across the hundred yards as rapidly as he did.

"No," I say, my voice trembling, "he missed."

Still staring at the body, I recognize the squared head of a viper. Lovely angular patterns adorn its muscular back, silver-grey, pale green, with hints of rose.

"She," Althea says.

Carefully, she lifts the body; it's still spasming futilely, the torn head dangling from its length. Gently, she finishes severing it.

"We'd best get away from this rock," she says. "There are probably young here, and their bite can be even more potent than hers."

The older woman has arrived. She reaches into her long dark skirt, pulls out the hem of a slip and steps out of it. She ties it off, forming a sack, then holds it open as Althea gently lowers the snake's body in. With precision, Althea picks up the head between her fingers.

"Thank you, sister," she says, laying it in the sack.

"Thank you," the older woman repeats, looking into

the bag.

With Matt's hand still on my shoulder, I walk back to the grove. I gladly take a drink of water, and find that my appetite has returned.

◆　◆　◆

We walk back to the long-buried wall, and sit.

Althea tells us how the war at last was brought to a conclusion.

"In the end,' she says, "it was decided not by strength but by cleverness.

"The attacking tribes had a shaman named Raven Eye. Like his totem animal, he knew the ways to bind trickery as well as to make it. He was of the same tribe as the Moon Princess, and was a counselor to her father. It was Raven Eye who had proposed making a pact among the suitors."

"At the sweat lodge," I say.

"Yes," she confirms. "And it was Raven Eye who proposed the final stratagem of the war."

It had become evident that the opponents were at a stalemate. The War Chief's party clearly had superior numbers, but the city people enjoyed two offsetting advantages — their defensive position, and their alliance with Horse, which enabled them to outmaneuver their attackers and ride them down in the open field.

Raven Eye suggested a peace offering.

The most skilled woodcarvers from the tribes of the war party went into the forest and created three dozen round, hollow masks of cedar, such as might sit atop a totem pole. Each showed Horse in one of her aspects — quietly grazing, or maternal, or alert and neighing, or running, or fierce and fighting, or asleep and dreaming ... Each mask, reaching nearly to the ground, would be worn by a single dancer, as in a longhouse ceremony.

"These are our horses," Raven Eye told the council. "Since we are not partners with Horse and her family, we will offer these as a gift to the city, to honor Horse and her superiority in battle."

The War Chief shook his head sadly.

"We have learned this," he said, "by great suffering. Indeed, we must honor Horse, and those who ride with her — for we cannot overcome them."

But honor, Althea says, arching an eyebrow, was not the only offering Raven Eye had in mind. The artisans also carved a secret chamber inside each mask, where weapons could be hidden. This peace offering, when accepted, would put three dozen armed men inside the city.

"In the quiet of the night, after the feasts and ceremonies, when all but the sentinels at the gates were sleeping, the dancers returned to their masks and armed themselves. Through the city they crept, with no noise but the owl's call, as they found and slew the city's warriors in their tents.

"One party stole into the chief's family tent and bound and kidnapped his daughters. Another found the Moon Princess. When awakened, she asked them not to bind her, and wept with relief that she was being freed."

The treacherous guests slipped out of the city through the lightly guarded north gate; before dawn, they were back in their camp, victorious.

The War Chief and his counselors had waited all night for them. As the sun rose, Raven Eye was still being carried on the shoulders of laughing, shouting men, as they told and retold the details of their successful exploit.

"But the same sun," the old woman says, "rose to reveal disaster in the city. Mothers and wives awoke to find their sons and husbands dead in their blood-soaked beds. Alarms and calls to arms mixed with wailing, as the chief and his people learned the extent of their losses.

"The city's chief, Bear Claw, knew they were beaten," the old woman says. "But his oldest son was unable to accept it, refused to surrender. Bear Claw had named this son Lodgepole: He was the tallest and sturdiest of his generation. But more importantly, his father had learned to rely on the young man's courage and resolve.

"So, at mid-day, he sent a mounted party to the attackers' camp, and proposed that they settle the war by single combat — between Lodgepole and any warrior of the attackers' choosing. He also asked for two nights and a day to bury and mourn the city's dead.

"That night and the next, Many Smokes filled the sky with its sorrow."

While the older woman has been speaking, the sun has touched the mountaintops and burst into flames of orange and pink; now it is sliding down behind them. Its dying lights inflame the clouds — crimson, orange, pale pink, and yellow, on smoky black — while patches of startlingly flat blue and blue-green tint the western sky. The eastern sky begins rapidly to darken, stretching up toward the fading west.

"We should head back," Althea says. "We can finish the story tonight."

Walking across the plateau, I turn back often to look at the fields and hills where the doomed city stood. I can still hear shrieks of grief and calls of alarm, from that morning so long ago.

♦ ♦ ♦

Deep dusk darkens the bluff's shadow, as we climb down toward the marsh; a rising evening mist makes soft, wet darkness. By the time we step onto the meadow grass, we cannot see our feet.

"Put your hand on my shoulder," Althea tells Matt. "My father was blind in his last years, and I long ago learned to find the way without seeing."

I put my hand in turn on Matt's shoulder.

"I have learned it, too," the old woman says, behind me. She does not take my shoulder.

We step along silently. The only sounds are the water's lapping, magnified in the moist air, and the call of an occasional bird. After we've gone a long while, the mist begins to thin out and I can see the grass-mounded ground; we're on a narrow, worn footpath.

Suddenly, just behind me, I hear a soft but heavy whooshing — a breeze ruffles my hair, and a huge shadow passes over. I duck, flinching.

Althea laughs softly.

Then the dim shape of the farmhouse emerges; on the eave above the door, a large white owl is just settling. It turns to regard us over its shoulder. As she opens the door, Althea reaches up and the bird steps gracefully down to her arm, opening its wide wings for balance.

"Go in and get warm," she says. "I will be a moment."

♦ ♦ ♦

Soon, holding mugs of hot soup by the fire, Matt and I are relaxing and listening to Althea's account of the war's last battle. The old woman has taken her soup back to the kitchen and begun preparing something else.

"The War Chief knew," Althea says, "there was only one warrior he could choose for the combat: Orca Smiling. But he also knew he might be refused if he asked privately — so he called a last war council, and let his chieftains make the choice."

She tells of the final encounter: The two champions facing each other on the wide plain, the city's whole population watching on one side, the attacking army on the other. As she narrates, describing each weapon, each stroke, each feint and counter-feint in the two-hour battle, Matt and I are drawn in; we hunch forward, our soup growing cold.

As she reaches the final, fateful blow, we're both holding our breath; we gasp to hear that they killed one another, Lodgepole driving an axe into Orca Smiling's chest, while the fatally wounded islander with his last strength heaved his dagger spear-like through his opponent's neck.

"All who had watched the battle, attackers and defenders alike, joined in the funerals, honoring their lost heroes," she says. "Orca Smiling's pyre was set at the water's edge at the southern end of the marsh, where his boats had been moored.

"The body of Lodgepole was burned atop the city's granary. Bear Claw told his people to divide into tribes and abandon the city at once. He and his chieftains and shamans had all agreed that this was no longer where the gods wanted them.

"So everyone left," Althea says. "The boats returned south and west, and the city's people once again took up their wandering. In a few days, where a city had long been, where a war had raged, the land was quiet. Only a few families remained, to fish and tend horses."

"And to tell the story," adds the old woman, carrying a steaming platter of rice and what looks like chicken, with vegetables adding green and red and yellow highlights. Despite the story's sad end, we are eager to eat after a day spent outdoors and hiking.

"Thank you again for feeding us," I say to the older woman.

"I only cooked," she says, as she heads back to the kitchen. "This time, it is you — and our sister — who have fed everyone."

She holds up the finely patterned snakeskin.

"Thank you again, sister," Althea says.

"Thanks, Dad," Matt whispers, smiling.

♦ ♦ ♦

In the morning, while mist is still rising from the water, Althea and Matt and I walk down to the marsh's southern end. Here, the strip of land narrows away until the bluff looms directly over the water.

At its foot, just where the land ends, stands an immense, twisting madrone tree. Its curving, silver-barked orange roots spring up from the sand as well as from a deep cleft in the bluff's face, and its trunk sweeps out over the water in a majestic cantilever, rising for fifty feet or more above the cliff top. In the morning light, the tree is afire with color — orange and silver, pink and grey, its branches shadowed in black and deep shades of green.

"This tree," Althea says, "grew on the spot where they burned Orca Smiling."

We are staring at it, imagining, remembering, when we hear the faint buzz of an engine. We turn, scanning the air and water.

"There," Matt says, pointing south.

A small, bird-size shape quickly grows as it moves toward us, soon becoming the flat-winged form of a seaplane. As it draws close it drops, one wing quickly dipping; the buzzing sound falls in pitch as the plane falls to the water. It lands and swiftly glides to where we stand.

Matt lifts his backpack and we walk out on a grassy spit of land. The plane's engine abruptly goes silent; it drifts toward us, turning at the last moment so its right pontoon gently bumps the shore. Matt reaches up and grabs a wing strut to still it.

On its side, I see a square, stylized figure: an eagle's head, a few black brushstrokes with a red-orange beak and eye. The pilot throws open the passenger door. Matt hoists his pack in, behind the empty seat, and turns to us.

"Thank you," he says to Althea, offering her an open hand.

"You are most welcome," she answers, laying her hand on his. With her other hand, she reaches into her pocket and gives him a small packet. It seems to be a golden scarf, the soft goat's wool she made our blankets from. Opening it, Matt finds a roll of snakeskin, several rattles still attached. He wraps it again, smiling.

"Thank you," he repeats.

He turns to me; we hug, hard.

"Goodbye, Dad," he says.

"Goodbye, Son," I say, holding the strong bulk of his body in my arms. "Thanks for coming here."

He turns and climbs into the plane, swinging the door shut.

The loud buzz erupts again, shattering the peace; the plane noses quickly away from the land, plows lightly across the water for a long hundred yards, then lifts into the air.

The wings dip a jaunty farewell.

When the plane has become a tiny white speck, hovering at the edge of vision, and its buzz is no louder than a mosquito's, Althea's hand touches my shoulder.

"I will go prepare the boat," she says. "Be there as soon as you can."


*I'm so proud of Matt, and I tell him that — yet I'm so worried for him, and I don't tell him that.*

*As a youth, I hurt and confused my own father by not wanting to go into the military, not even considering the Navy that had been both home and father to him in his youth.*

*I know this story, too well.*

*But I wonder: Does Matt?*

*How much have I actually told him?*

*From time to time, on vacations or weekend drives, we'd pass near the California Maritime Academy, its ship moored beside the Vallejo Bridge, and I'd remind the kids that granddad went there. Did I ever say that he wanted me to go too? That I didn't? And that it hurt his feelings? Or did I only think it?*

*Silence. Our family curse.*

*My father never talked at all about his wars — World War II, Korea. They were a huge part of his life, the scenes where he became an adult. And others have told what a trial by fire war is, how deeply it scars ...*

*Yet nothing.*

*In the half-century he lived after his wars were over, he never told a story, shared a memory. Only a humorous tale or two that he and my mother would recount together, things they did when he and a pal were home on shore leave.*

*A few years ago, after Dad was gone, I heard from an old friend of his that one of the "Liberty ships" Dad served on — they were old merchant junkers, or new "tin cans" slapped together to carry munitions and supplies — had been sunk in the Pacific, and Dad was among the handful who survived.*

*But from him, silence.*

*Dad and Matt treasured their times together. Did they share stories of life in the military? Did they talk of living under the daily threat of death?*

*Did Dad ever drop a dark hint (as he was so fond of doing) about how bitterly disappointed he was in me?*

*What do I tell, what do I keep to myself?*

Walking by the madrone tree, I pick up a curl of its weathered silver bark and carry it.

As I near the farmhouse, I see my backpack leaning in the doorway. And something's on top of it — a small bundle, blue-grey.

By the time I pick it up, I know it is Althea's goat's wool. Inside the scarf lies a small, white, squarish skull; its eye sockets are empty, its jaws delicately hinged. Two fangs curve menacingly down from the upper jaw. A golden chain loops through the skull.

I unzip my jacket, slip open the chain's catch, lift it around my neck, and close it. The bone rests light on my chest, just below my throat, and I can feel the feather-like tip of each fang.

I smile.

"Thank you, sister," I say.

Wrapping the scarf around my neck, I cross its ends over the skull and zip my jacket. I pick up my pack and head for the dock.

The boat is facing seaward now, the stern line holding it. I unloop the line from the piling and step in, lowering my pack and sitting.

"Thank you," I say to the silent, hooded figure in the bow who seems to be meditating or praying, and does not turn. If there is an answer, I cannot hear it over the coughing of the outboard motor as I fire it up.

Soon, we are gliding between the snags, toward open

water. For perhaps two hours, we sail south and a little west in silence. Wind and water, and an occasional gull cry, are the only sounds.

*The water's rushing feels like it's my life slipping by. I don't know anything anymore.*

*What is it to be a man? A father? Is it loving? Is it letting go?*

*Is everything I've done and felt — is it wrong? Wanting to be the one who held them, who loved them, who shielded them, who taught them ...*

*For years I was that. Or tried to be. And then I suddenly became ... the one who went away. Who abandoned them? Who didn't love them enough to stay?*

*A gull cries, and it sounds to me like it's laughing at the bitter joke: It was because I loved them that I left.*

*I don't know if I ever would have let myself see how bad our marriage had become. At first sexless, then affectionless, then not conversing or sharing at all, just ships passing in the night.*

*I don't know if I ever would have acted for myself, to save my heart, my life.*

*The change was gradual, over several years. So gradual it was impossible to notice. Phoebe sank deeper and deeper (into what we learned years later was severe bipolar disorder), and I sank with her. We slipped, day by unwitting day, into grey limbo, into exhaustion.*

*Without understanding it, unable to mark the change by pointing to an event, our family's life fell into the shadows. We all shaped ourselves to her engulfing weeks and months of depression, her brief spurts of creative — or at times, alas, rageful — energy.*

*I could feel something awful was happening, or had happened, but I didn't know what it could be. I kept feeling that whatever it was, it must be my fault, or at least my responsibility. I was supposed to find some way to make it better. But I kept failing.*

*Then Phoebe's outbursts of wrath began to fall on Matt, a shy and slender 12-year-old. And I knew I had to act. At my insistence, we met with a therapist. In a two-hour session, we agreed that I should rent a room or apartment while we worked out how to heal our marriage — or build a new one. Two days later, Phoebe handed me divorce papers.*

*In a moment, everything I had spent the last twenty years living for was gone. It had fallen down around me, as if our house had burned down while I stood in it.*

*I was numb for weeks. Months. I walked through the endless days not even half-awake, focusing only on the next thing, the next task. I felt like I was again a child, learning to walk through the San Francisco fog — my head down, trying to make out the sidewalk, trying not to be afraid.*

*In our early years together, Phoebe and I used to read stories together at bedtime. One told of a family of rabbits, who would go into a state called "tharn" if a predator appeared. They'd go suddenly silent, immobile, unable to think or to act or (mercifully) to feel.*

*I thought I was doing alright, finding my way one day at a time. I didn't realize I had "gone tharn" —and how it insulated me from feeling.*

*One by one the losses came, like slashes of a predator's claw — stripping away where I lived, who I loved, who loved me ... There's almost no way to survive such an onslaught of loss, as it crashes over you relentlessly, wave after wave. I had a mantra in those days: "The only way out is through." And "tharn" was the only way through.*

*Living numb, it turns out, doesn't leave you too many memories.*

*I know the landmarks ... moving out, moving into a new place, then another ... I know the steps in the long, achingly slow court process ... filling out forms, trying to put abysmal pain into words for strangers, sorting out our shattered family as if we were a roomful of objects ... I know things that happened, things that must have taken place ...*

*But I can't recall many scenes or moments from those months.*

*I do recall one: stones and small plants, scattered along a path leading up a desert mountainside.*

*Shadow Mountain arose from the middle of a neighborhood a mile from our house — the house where we last lived together. One of Matt's school friends lived there, and from time to time, the kids and I had clambered up its slopes on weekend romps.*

*This time, I was climbing alone, head down, looking for clues. Phoebe had called, worried, to say Matt was gone. He'd been away for two days and nights, and she couldn't find him at any of his friends' houses.*

*So, I called in to my day job sick and spent the day trying to find him — an angry, terrified boy, who'd fled from home after another loud fight with his mother. I could sense that he didn't want to be found, but also that he did. And I guessed that he probably was alone, not wanting to have to tell anyone what was going on in his family.*

*I spent a couple of hours driving, up and down streets and alleys, hoping against the odds to catch a glimpse of him. Then I drove past the mountain, and heard his voice saying, "Dad, some day we should bring our sleeping bags here and stay overnight."*

*I parked and began a slow ascent, peering into the trailside rubble and the scrawny weeds, looking for signs. Near the summit, on a shelf of small gravel and sand, I thought I saw the place where a body had lain.*

*Had this been Matt? Or perhaps a homeless person? I realized, with a dry laugh, that he was homeless, too.*

*Walking back downhill, I felt encouraged; I was pretty sure he'd spent the night here. But I wondered where to look next.*

*Rounding the last hummock, I could see the parking lot. There he was, leaning against the car, his backpack on the hood.*

*"Hi, Dad," he said.*

*We hugged.*

*"I went by Dave's, but he's at school. I came back here, 'cause I didn't know where else to go. Then I saw your car."*

*After a conference with his mother, Matt came to live with me, and I looked for a larger apartment.*

There's that memory. A few others.

But mostly there's just a haze, a dull fog I can't see through.

It's hard to believe almost two years went by that way. But they did.

By the time I felt I was back in my life, alive and able to remember, things had changed.

I was still a full-time father to Matt, but only a weekend father for the three younger kids — without a house of my own, bringing them to our small apartment with its poorly tended pool. Taking them to eat at pizza parlors and burger joints. I remember crying at a movie about men who called themselves "McDaddies," because they met their ex-wives to exchange the children at fast-food outlets.

I felt like I was fast food for the younger three, wrapping myself up in quick packages to hand them. All the long, slow luxury of living together was gone. It had to be crammed into a few hours, an overnight.

*What kind of nourishment did they get from me in those frantic weekends? We spent half our time in the car, rushing back and forth between their home and "your place," "the apartment."*

Eventually, I was no longer numb. But now I felt pain, constant pain. And I felt rootless, torn from the ground.

I guess I still do.

*Chapter 4*

## OWL ISLAND

We approach a barren-looking island. It has patches of trees at its summits, and thin grasses and exposed rocks over most of its surface. It seems out of place amid the region's misty, forested islands.

We land at a rock jetty beside a small harbor, a mile or so south of the island's northern tip. Ours is the only boat.

As we tie off the lines, my companion's hood falls open and I am shocked — it is not Althea's short dark hair I see but long, red-gold tresses. She turns, for the first time looking at me; it is my older daughter.

"Em!"

I'm speechless. We haven't talked in months, and she hasn't written in more than a year.

"Hello, Dad," she says. She continues looking at me as I step toward her, unsure how to greet her. She smiles, holding out her arms. I gladly hug her.

"Thank you for coming," I say. "I didn't —"

"I know," she says.

She steps back to the boat, picks up two packs and hands me mine. I follow her toward the land.

There is no one to greet us as we walk up the hillock behind the harbor. Emma seems to know what she's looking for. She's always seemed to know what she's looking for. In sixth grade, she had her high school chosen; in high school, she had picked her college. The one time she changed direction was to change majors from journalism to theatre. She made the change comfortably, and was doing well in her junior year when her mother became ill, and she had to drop out. Six months later, when she returned to college, she had a more practical goal: teaching. Which she was now doing with a program for under-served youth.

Emma strides easily up the hillside. I'm struck, as always, by her beauty: just above medium height, her frame a bit more solid than slim, her body long since enriched into a woman's. Her hair, released, falls lightly down her back, strands lifting in the late morning breeze.

*I remember seeing the first tendrils of Emma's hair — pasted wet to her tiny head, crowning that magnificent new face we'd waited so many months to see. I'm still amazed as I recall her smiling up, eyes already open, seconds after she emerged from her mother's body. I felt I was assisting at the world's creation.*

*I also remember feeling something deep within me being pulled, tugged by the open place above her lip, where the tissue hadn't closed.*

*"Oh child," I whispered, "I swear to you — you will always know you are loved, and beautiful."*

*And I remember the most surprising part of that moment, Emma's first in this world. How her presence suddenly touched — and ended — something in me: a deep loneliness, so profound I never until that moment knew I'd been feeling it. Yet I'd been living under the weight of it all my life.*

*I never told Em — or anyone — about this. I didn't understand it, and I couldn't imagine anyone else would. But looking at her, as she lay in my arms, I heard the words as if they'd been spoken aloud:*

*"You're not alone any more. At last, there's another one of your kind on this planet."*

*I know many men feel a strong desire for a son, someone "to carry on the family name." I'd never felt that, nor understood it at all.*

*And this was my daughter ...*

*She was my first-born. That was important in the Bible, and in fairy tales. Was that maybe it? Was I responding to some ancient archetype or image? I didn't know.*

*I did know I was totally unprepared for this. I had no idea that holding my newborn daughter might utterly change my life.*

*Oh, people talked endlessly about how having an infant to care for will turn your daily life upside down.*

*But I couldn't remember anyone saying that this tiny new person, whose entire body could rest on my forearm, might bring a message, as if from another world ... might shift how my life felt deep inside, privately. Might shift it more than anything I'd ever experienced.*

*I'd never heard that this could happen. Nor that it might be normal.*

*So I spent years worrying that it wasn't. I feared that something was wrong with me, and that maybe this intense bond I felt with Emma was unfair to the other children, or emotionally dangerous for her.*


When we reach the hilltop, we can see a long, flat valley stretching north and south below us. Em points to the right.

"That's where we go," she says.

We begin stepping carefully down the dry slope, trying not to slip in the loose scree of rock shards or dislodge the tufts of grass that sprout here and there among them. Not far from the hill's base, we find a well-worn track and turn north, still alone on this strangely quiet land.

♦  ♦  ♦


"Welcome to Owl Island," says a young woman, rising from her seat on a rock by the road as we draw near. She is the first person we have seen.

"I am Dora. I'll take you to my grandfather."

Her features are wide and rounded, as is her body, and her skin is teak-brown. Her dark hair is wound up in coiled braids, under a wide straw hat.

She leads us off the road, across a meadow of sparse grass where scattered groups of sheep are grazing. A stiffness in her left knee gives her a slightly rolling gait, yet she moves quickly and surely through the rocky field. Sheep look up as she walks past, and they move toward her expectantly. She speaks a few words to them, tapping her stout, curved walking stick on the ground, and they stop, then return to grazing.

After a few minutes, we have climbed a modest ridge and are walking through the woods along its crest. I'm grateful for the shade, as the sun has reached the top of the sky. Ahead of us, in the trees, she indicates a small log cabin beside a brook; beyond it, the woods end and a wide flat ledge extends, ringed by a low rock wall.

I recognize it as the sheep pen. A figure is sitting on the rock wall, robed in black and wearing another of the flat straw hats, looking down the hillside away from us.

"Yaya," the girl calls, and the figure turns. "Here they are."

By its slow, careful rising, the body of a very old man reveals itself. We draw near, and are introduced.

"This is my grandfather, Reader," she says. I cannot help noticing that the old man's eyes, apparently once dark blue, are clouded grey with cataracts.

"Not of books," she adds, catching my look.

"Signs," the old man says, with a dry laugh. "I am the Reader of Signs for this generation. It has been my gift ... or curse ... since my youth.

"Look," he adds, pointing down the hillside where he has been watching. A half-mile away, nestled at the foot of the hills, lies a sizeable community, with tile-roofed stone dwellings and a wide main street, as well as several small alleys.

"Owl Village. We will go there this evening for the story dancing. For now, come, let us get out of the sun."

He leads us to the cabin's wide front porch, where there are hand-made wooden benches. Sitting on them, we can look across to the sheep pen, and down upon the village. His granddaughter brings blue glasses and two tall pitchers, then excuses herself to return to tending the sheep.

"If I were young," the old man says, "I would say that our story, the one you will see enacted tonight by the dancers, is a story of pride. Pride that has wasted our land, made it all but barren.

"But now I do not know what I would say. What makes pride?" He looks at each of us. "What wound is it that cannot heal? Or what healing makes the skin so brittle that any touch is felt as a blow?"

His gaze turns back toward the distant village.

"Once long ago," he says, "our people were many, and we were wealthy and comfortable. Indeed, our chief was traditionally called Father of Herds, for the many animals our people tended, roaming the rich green fields and woodlands that were here. But the last chief of that name was a father of a different sort.

"Perhaps it was the war. He had gone to be a suitor for the Moon Princess, and became a brother to the other suitors. As a brother, he had taken part in the war at Many Smokes. There, like every warrior, he experienced things ... things no man can safely do or bear.

"Yet when he returned, all seemed well. Within the year he married, to a princess from the valley clans who served them as Priestess of the Seeds, an honor held by the women of her family for generations. Soon, the bride grew large with their first child. The Reader of that time studied the signs and said their child would be a son, and would become an even greater chief than his father.

"But this news did not please Father of Herds. Instead, he became anxious and unable to sleep at night, and when the child was born, he ordered the midwife to tie the infant's legs together and cast him into the sea."

The old man sighs, and sips from his glass.

"The midwife knew she could not do this. While the chief watched, she ticd the baby's legs together with a leather thong. But the basket she chose to carry him in was a water basket — tightly woven and lined with pitch, to make it waterproof. When she got to the sea's edge, she set the child afloat, calling to the Sea People to take him and safeguard him.

*We were sea people when I was small.*

*I grew up next to the Pacific Ocean.*

*I remember standing ankle-deep in the cold surf, casting out heavily weighted lines and then slowly reeling them back in, listening with our fingers for sea bass or perch to hit the bait, tug at the line.*

*I remember my father laughing like a boy while he climbed up the wave-crashed rocks, his heavy peacoat swinging about him, looking for a better spot to cast from.*

*The sea was his second home.*

*At 17, he'd left Chicago's suburbs to join his brother in the Navy. It gave him a paycheck to send his mother. And it gave him a father. A father to replace the one who'd disappeared one morning out his office window when the Depression hit.*

*Out on the sea, in a ship, the boy from Chicago lived*

*in a world of men. Men who fiercely taught him how to be one of them.*

"Among those who heard was Seal. She summoned a couple who had no pups, and they swam with the basket, pushing it to the rock they called home, where they took the child and raised him. They hastily chewed the thong off his ankles, but the sea water had made it tighten cruelly, cutting the flesh and tendons deeply.

"The boy was thus slow to learn walking; but they did not mind, for they could not walk either. And he was otherwise a beautiful and healthy child. He learned quickly to swim and catch fish, and gave them years of pleasure, while they gave him much love and tender teaching.

"But of course, as he grew older, he grew to look more and more unlike them, and became curious about his own kind. Finally, one day, as they were watching the two-leggeds fishing in their boats, he knew he was of that people, and he asked to go and seek his place among them. With many tears, they parted."

The old man stops and refills our glasses.

"Here," he says. "I am sorry — I have not even invited you to freshen yourselves after your journey. I have just started talking, boring you with what interests an old man."

We both decline his offer, insisting that we'd prefer to hear more. It's restful to sit on the shaded porch and watch the peaceful view, sipping cool drinks and listening. Blue jays are chatting in the afternoon light, jumping through the air from branch to branch, and a large red squirrel sits in a pine above us, chipping away at a cone.

"Well," he says, "it may help you to understand what you will see tonight. After all, our people know these stories from childhood, hearing them told and watching them danced year after year.""

He tells us how the young man gingerly entered into the world of humans — at first peering from behind rocks and bushes, then at last coming forward and introducing himself to a herdsman.

He tells us how the people were astonished by the boy's appearance, barely clothed, his chest and arms made large by a life of swimming and diving. With such muscles in his upper body, people took him for a champion — and indeed, he turned out to be as skillful in feats of strength as he was at swimming.

"The name they gave him was an ancient word for a swelling, because his body seemed so swollen up," he says. "It was the same word used for the swelling of a wave, so it always carried the echo of his life in the sea."

"Well," Emma says, smiling, "with his strength, and his coming from the sea, I'd call him Breaker."

"Ha!" the old man laughs. "Wonderful! Breaker. For us, that will be his name. Breaker." He nods and chuckles. "This is a better name than you know," he says, regarding her closely for a moment. Then he takes a drink, and resumes his tale.

Young Breaker's friends were eager to enter him in the harvest games, to which all the villages on the island — and several on nearby islands — sent competitors. The harvest festival, a celebration of fertility, was also the time for blessing the year's marriages. And the athlete who was crowned champion would join the Priestess of the Seeds as her ritual mate for the day, blessing the new-made couples and the land.

"This was the honor Breaker's friends sought for him," the old man says.

"But unknown to anyone, our chief, Father of Herds, decided to disguise himself and enter as a contestant in that year's games. He was too old for such doings, but something clouded his judgment."

"Pride?" I offer.

"Whatever it was, I think it was the same thing that made him fearful of being succeeded by a son," the old man answers, shaking his head.

*As a boy, I learned to love the sea.*

*The greatest privilege was being invited aboard one of my father's ships. Once, I even got to spend three days aboard a refitted destroyer, as it made a "shakedown" cruise from San Francisco to Monterey and back.*

*However, having the Navy for a grandfather was a mixed blessing.*

*My father was by nature loving and playful. But he had learned to obey and believe in a rigid military discipline. When his wife gave him two sons to raise, he tried to make our house into an orderly ship, with himself as its captain.*

*My mother had no such idea. He hadn't been present for either of our births, and like most sailors' wives, she had grown used to running the home, making all the decisions on her own, during his long absences.*

*Also like most sailor's wives, she held his soft, feeling self in her keeping while he was at sea. When he was ashore, he wanted that self back. He wanted to play with her, be her lover and her boyfriend, and even — in private moments — her little boy.*

*He also relied on her as the lead partner in dealing with the brave new world of homeowning and parenting, of which he knew nothing — not as an obedient junior officer.*

*So our home was pulled back and forth, like the sea under the inconstant moon. At some times, we shared love and laughter, gentleness and play; at other times, we heard barked orders and cruel nicknames, and my brother and I felt the wide leather Navy belt bite into our bare legs and bottoms.*

*At night, looking out our bedroom window at the moon, listening to the surf's rush and return, I could feel that tugging inside me. And I felt confused. I knew my father loved me, and I wanted him to — but why did he also hate me?*

"As the masked contestant," the old man says, "Father of Herds won many events. So did Breaker. Indeed, had his weak ankles not kept him out of the foot races, Breaker would easily have been named the champion. As it was, the two of them led the field; everyone saw that one or the other would be crowned.

"Then, in the stone tossing, the unknown one went first. He picked up a boulder the weight of man and hurled it far, almost three body lengths. When it landed, it narrowly missed young Breaker, who had to leap aside to save his life.

"From the masked one's laughter, it was clear he was

not surprised — nor sorry. Then Breaker went to the line and lifted up his stone, and hurled it. It landed directly on top of the other stone, shattering it. And a huge piece flew out, striking the unknown contestant and breaking his skull.

"The gathered tribes were aghast. Father of Herds was dead. The games were ended at once; the harvest festival, always a time of joy and revelry, became instead an elaborate funeral.

"Still, it was necessary to bless the marriages and the land. After the funeral, when it came time for this, the widowed Priestess of the Seeds was in seclusion, mourning. Because he was the champion, and thus her ceremonial mate for the day, young Breaker went to her and begged her forgiveness. In tears, he pleaded with her to carry out their ritual duty for the well-being of the earth and the people.

"With his encouraging, she found the heart and strength to do this. Somberly, leaning on his arm, she completed the rituals. And the people went home, knowing that in the coming year, their fields and families would prosper."

The old man stops, looking at the western sky, which is beginning its symphony of deep, dramatic colors.

"Ah! I am sorry," he says, pushing himself up off the bench. "Now you will have no rest at all. And I have not even finished the story. But as soon as the sun is set, the dancing will begin, so I must make a little haste to get you there. You may want warm clothing; the village will be cool tonight."

Silver light pours down on us from a round moon riding low above the ridge; the copper gleams from Emma's hair. We are standing in the village square. Flat wagons full of bundled children line the edges of the plaza, adults standing everywhere in front of them. Drums and flutes weave the air full of music.

In the middle, on a platform of pounded earth edged in brick, dancers are acting out what the old man has told us. He stands with us, wrapped in a poncho of dark blue, murmuring his commentary.

"Puffed up," he notes, as colorful balloon-like sacs hidden in the shirt of a boy dancer, portraying young Breaker, slowly inflate. "His ancient name."

The dancer is moving sinuously with a male and female in silky black and brown, who wear whiskered, large-eyed masks — his seal parents.

Children giggle gleefully as the bright-striped balloons expand.

When the seal dancers leave, an older male dancer, wearing an identically colored and inflated shirt, changes places with the boy.

He dances in a series of contests with other male dancers. Again and again, he is engaged by one dancer who wears an expressionless round mask before his face. Suddenly that dancer falls, and the round mask drops off; beneath it is the silver-bearded face of a mature chief.

We then watch the funeral dance, as the fallen dancer is carried on the others' shoulders.

After the funeral dance, we share a quiet meal, as do the families all around the edges of the square.

I remember, with some shame, how I gradually moved away from my father, and toward my mother.

As a teenager, I had started writing poetry. I was also spending my high school summers happily ensconced in a theater program at the local college, where my parents had both gone back to school.

My father was glad to listen to my poems, and enthusiastically applauded each play I was in. But my mother would talk about them in detail with me. And when she brought home the stories she was writing for her classes, the two of us would sit for hours, going over them line by line — something she never did with my father.

When it was time for me to think of college, my parents helped me apply to all the best ones, and for the scholarships that would enable me to go. Neither of them urged me to stay within our means and go to the local college.

But my father did make it clear that he could imagine no finer place for his son's education than the US Naval Academy. Or, nearer home, the shipboard curriculum at California's Maritime Academy.

But I had come to fear — and even let myself feel hot anger at — the military regime that kept invading our home. I wanted to get away from it, and avoid it forever.

It didn't occur to me then, but now I wonder whether my father was perplexed — hurt, even — that his firstborn son wasn't the least bit interested in following his footsteps. This boy, who so loved life on board ship, and who felt so at home on the sea or even along its edges ...

When the meal is done, the dancers resume the story.

We watch the blessing of the land, and of the year's bridal couples. The widowed priestess wears her crown of woven grasses and fruits, accompanied by the colorfully shirted Breaker.

Then the harvest dances erupt. By the time they have ended, younger children are nodding and yawning in the trucks and wagons.

There is one more dance. It begins with a duet between Breaker and the widowed priestess.

"He was such a comfort to her," the old man murmurs, "that at the next harvest festival, they too were married."

Young dancers appear, one by one, on the stage with them, until there are four, two boys and two girls. One of the girls wears a small crown of red-gold grasses like her mother's.

The family dances together. Other groups join them, each wearing a different color. Soon, the stage is filled with dancers in interlocking wheels, all turning slowly clockwise.

"During Breaker's years as chief," the old man says, "the island's tribes became unified, and prospered as never before.

"But then, suddenly, a plague struck our island."

Dancers in grey enter. Each carries a cloth effigy and weaves through the circles, which grow still. Each lays its effigy at the feet of Breaker and the priestess.

A tall figure in black, with an eyeless mask, enters and lays his hands on their shoulders.

"The Reader," the old man says.

The music stops.

The Reader kneels, lifts the hem of Breaker's costume, and exposes his ankles. They are wrapped in red and black rags.

The priestess cries out, a single awful note, and collapses. The drums begin to race; Breaker rushes toward her.

The Reader stops him and makes him watch her — a silent dance, a dance of agony, of love, and of hopeless grief. She is telling him what she now knows: She is his mother.

The drums rap sharply; the four children fall to the ground.

Breaker leaps from the platform, caught by the dancers in grey, who raise bright green knives and slash at him, loudly bursting the colorful balloons of his costume.

Above and behind them, the priestess lifts a long silver knife and slays herself.

"When she died," the old man says, "he threw himself off a cliff, and landed in thorn bushes. They found him still alive — but blind."


*Well, I think, there's a story.*

*A boy who overcomes his jealous, fearful father and wins his mother for a mate.*

*Yes, it applies to me. Far more than I wish it did. It calls to mind a dream that shocked me — and embarrassed me — in college. One hot afternoon, the phone jarred me out of a deep sleep to realize that I'd been having a very erotic shower with my mother.*

*So I was like Breaker.*

*But why am I here with Emma, watching this story acted out?*

Breaker, his costume in tatters, struggles to his knees. Red ribbons now hang from his eyes.

The four children also rise. One girl leads the two boys off. The other girl, the one with the gold circlet, goes to Breaker and lifts him to his feet.

"His older daughter, Little Mother," the old man says. "She became his eyes."

Hobbling, leaning on her arm, Breaker follows Little Mother around the square. Flutes play sadly, slowly.

*Oh my god.*

*She is a girl of no more than seven.*

*Did I do that? Have I blindly depended on my daughter? Have I been a weight she must carry?*

*I see Emma, at that very age.*

*Her hair flies out behind her as she runs down the driveway to greet me. I am coming home from my day job, at our last house. She throws her arms around me, jumping up into mine.*

*I am delighted, as always, to see her.*

*But this time, in this moment of simple joy, I also feel something off, not quite right, like a single note gone wrong in the harmony of a song. Walking into the house, for the first time I let myself admit that something is wrong in our home.*

*Beside my love for Em, I can feel that I am starting to count on her daily greeting and conversation. To rely on it for something I've long been missing from Phoebe, who lies sick in bed.*

*I don't know what ails Phoebe, and I'm at my wits' end trying to find what I can do to make things right for her, for us. But all at once I know one thing for certain: This way of living will not be good for Emma. It has to change.*

Suddenly, as Breaker and his daughter circle the plaza, objects start flying at them from the crowd. Landing, they sound like shattering clay or clattering wood.

"Every broken thing," the old man says. "His actions, you see, broke the sacred laws. This is why *your* name for him," he looks at Emma, "was so well given.

"Each year, he takes with him all the things of each household that have broken and cannot be mended. Pots, bowls, cups, tools — everything."

Grey-clad dancers carrying large sacks begin gathering up the broken items. They follow the pair around the plaza three times, then leave.

The musicians begin a final chant.

"Tomorrow," the old man says, shifting in his poncho, "the procession begins at sunrise. It will travel the length of our island, to Oyster Village, at the southern tip. There, the ceremonies will be completed."

He turns and starts back toward his cabin. As we pass through the dispersing crowd, he exchanges quiet embraces with many of the people.

♦ ♦ ♦

Before the dawn light, I am already up and sitting on the porch, awakened by dreams. I don't remember them, but the disturbance they have created stays with me.

*It's so hard to know what to tell children when your marriage is over.*

*You don't want to blame the other parent — even if you're angry and feel blindsided. You don't want to explain a failed sex life to them, or the slow death of intimacy. (Even if you wanted to, how would you begin to explain what you yourself can't understand?)*

*So there I was, the four of them clustered around me on the couch, letting them know their world was about to fall apart. I don't recall what words I chose, or how they asked what they needed to ask.*

*I know it ended with tears, from all of us. And with me promising that their mother and I would always love them, no matter where any of us might live.*

*And what comfort, I wondered sadly, could that be at this moment?*

*Several months later, when spring returned, I bought an inflatable swimming pool. By then, visits to a family therapist were part of our weekend routine. The pool was Anne's idea.*

*"They're feeling some anger," she'd said. "A lot, in fact. But they love you too much to show it. They're afraid to hurt you — and afraid you might leave."*

*Pierced and shamed, but hopeful, I took us to the mall. While I looked at plastic pools, Carlie found an inflated doll, the kind you push down and it pops back upright. It was as tall as she was, taller than Timmy.*

*"Pow!" I heard — I turned, and Carlie had slammed the doll backward. It fell to the floor and bounced back up, and she slugged it again.*

*"Pow!" she shouted again, as Timmy laughed.*

*My god, I thought, Anne was so right — and before I could finish the thought, the doll had popped up again.*

*Carlie flew at it, both fists flying.*

*"Don't you ever say that about my dad!" she growled.*

*An hour later, I sat on the patio, blowing lungfuls of air into the flat shape.*

*Eventually, while the hose filled the pool, we all got in. I gently splashed Tim, as Anne had suggested. He hesitated, then splashed me back, laughing. Soon, he and Carlie and I were splashing up waves at each other.*

*Then I heard Carlie say, "Ohhh" — and a bucket of water came pouring down on my head. Behind me, Emma's gleeful, throaty cackle rang out.*

I'm sitting with these thoughts when I hear an owl call; another one answers. Sheep rustle in their pen.

A small bell rings out, twice, and I hear someone stirring. I wonder if our host uses an alarm clock, then a figure steps out the door, talking softly.

It is Emma, talking into a cell phone in her left hand.

91

She's wearing a long nightgown, her jacket wrapped over it. She startles a bit when she sees me, then smiles. I walk down the steps off the porch, to give her some privacy.

Standing at the dark wood's edge, leaning against a tree, I see her barely visible outline and hear the soft, familiar murmur of her voice.

The owls call again.


*I remember a day when she was 13, and we all went swimming in the pool at the townhouse I now lived in. After showering, Em came down the stairs wearing one of my T-shirts, brushing her hair, her emerging body giving the shirt a slight shape it had never had before.*

*Later, while the other children slept, Emma and I talked. I told her I was pleased to see her body changing.*

*She blushed, and ducked her head.*

*I said that as it changed, she'd find her body affecting people in ways it hadn't before.*

*"You mean sex, Dad?" She gave me a tolerant smile. "I've had health class, y'know."*

*"Yes," I laughed, "I do know. And I do mean that from now on, your beauty will be in part sexual. In part. But mostly, it will still be because of who you are, your soul and your personality, shining through into the world. Like always."*

*She half-ducked her head, but didn't break eye contact.*

*"As your dad, I want to be sure you're aware of that. And I want you to be the one who's in control of*

*how your beauty is expressed."*

*Her brow furrowed. "You mean, like clothes and makeup?"*

*"Yes, and how you use your body. With TV and music videos and movies, and everyone wanting to sell you something —"*

*"This is cool, that's in style," she said, nodding.*

*"It's so easy to get swept up in it all, and lose sight of who you are, how you want to be seen and treated ..."*

*"Yeah. You know, Dad, Mom and I do talk about this a lot, how you want to be seen. Especially when we're going shopping. Carlie, too."*

*"I'm glad," I said. "I knew she'd taught you to be great bargain hunters ..."*

*"Yeah, but Mom's all about getting classics, things that look good — and last for more than a season. Though I guess we haven't talked as much about the sex part ..."*

*"Well, you can always talk about it with me. The 'sex part' of life can get pretty confusing. Nobody knows how to handle it all, so we learn by trying, and by making mistakes ..."*

*"OK," she said.*

*"Enough for now?"*

*"Yeah. And Dad —"*

*"Huh?"*

*"Thanks."*

"Dad?" Her voice calls softly from the porch.

93

"Right here," I say, going back to the stairs.

"Looks like I'll have to leave sooner than I thought. One of our staff is ill, and I have to fill in. I'll have to be at Bear Island before two, to catch a ferry. I'll need the boat, but I'll leave it for you. It'll be at Two Moon Harbor."

"Okay," I say, taken aback. "I can do that. I'm sure sorry to lose you so soon."

"Me too," she says. We stand, looking at each other quietly for a moment. A dawn breeze brushes over us, chilling our shoulders, shaking the boughs in a gentle whisper. The sheep stir, baa-ing softly, and the owls call and answer once more. Then other birds begin to sing in the softening darkness.

"I guess it's time to get ready," she says, pulling the screen door open.

◆ ◆ ◆

The sun sits well above deep green mountains to the east — the high backbone of Bear Island, perhaps two miles away. We're walking south, down the long central valley of Owl Island.

For today's performance, there are several dozens of us in a loose procession, led by Breaker and Little Mother (now being danced by a young woman). After them come the musicians, a dozen grey-clad dancers with bags over their shoulders, and families trailing after. We also seem to have attracted a posse of grey and yellow dogs, who trot along with us eagerly.

Here and there, people stand beside the wide road, waiting. As Breaker passes, they toss their broken bowls and implements at him. He does not attempt to duck but acknowledges them, humbly. The dancers in grey pick up what's been thrown. A long cloud of dust angles up into the air behind us, obscuring the view of where we have been.

In about an hour, we reach a fork in the road, where it parts around a clump of sturdy oaks. The procession continues south, taking the right branch; Dora, the Reader's granddaughter, motions Emma and me to one side, under the oaks.

"From here," she tells Emma, pointing west, "keep that square boulder lined up with the notch up on the ridge. Walk toward it. When you reach the notch, look down to your left, and you'll see your boat."

"Thank you," Em says.

"Thank you for coming," Dora answers, smiling. "And good sailing."

I open my arms to hug Em goodbye. Though our backpacks make us awkward, we manage an embrace.

"Goodbye, love," I say. "I can't tell you what it means that you came."

"Goodbye, Dad," she says. "Good luck."

I feel a sudden wrenching in my chest as she walks away, her red-gold hair wound up in a loose bun, a few strands trailing over her pack. Twice, she turns and waves.

I want to watch until she reaches the boulder, until she crests the ridge and disappears downhill toward the harbor, until I can see her no more. But before she has gone even halfway to the rock, I feel a hand on my shoulder.

I turn and Dora smiles, nodding gently.

*Emma has always been good at sensing when she needs to withdraw, to get on with her priorities. She doesn't let herself be held captive, hostage to someone else's need or expectation. In a conversation ... or, in her school years, when she'd announce that she had homework and head off to her room ...*

*Even in affairs of the heart ...*

*I remember worrying that Tom, the fellow she was with the longest, might blackmail her into accepting an "open" relationship when their jobs took them to different cities. But Emma voiced her limits, and stood firm, even though the cost was painful.*

*I wish I'd had that skill at her age.*

*Now Em's on her way back to her life, and I'm on this road alone.*

*Though Dora is with me. And I'd have no way of knowing what to do if she weren't.*

It's past midday, and hot on the road. There is no place to stop or drink, and we're dusty and tired. The dogs are panting, tongues hanging out.

I remember the water bottle Tim put in my pack, and swing the pack off my shoulders. Finding the bottle, I offer it to Dora, while I work my arms back into the straps.

"Drink," I say. "Please."

"Wait," she says. "We should do this first."

She half-trots around the others, toward the front of the procession. She reaches the dancers, unstops the bottle, and offers it to Little Mother. Dust-streaked, eyes half-glazed, her gold circlet askew in her hair, the dancer looks at Dora.

"Who are you?" she asks.

"I am a father's daughter," Dora says.

Little Mother nods, accepts the bottle, and takes a brief pull.

"Thank you, sister," she says, wiping it off and handing it back. "I am you."

Then Dora returns and hands me the bottle, tilting her head toward Breaker.

He is a sturdy man, twenty years younger than I, but I can see that he is deeply tired, moving almost unconsciously, needing Little Mother's shoulder to keep him upright. Scratches and cuts mark his face and arms where broken objects have hit him.

One cut, on his right cheek, has bled quite a bit and has left his shirt and skin — and the red ribbon hanging from his brow — caked with dry, dusty blood.

I hand him the bottle.

"Who are you?" he asks.

"I ... I am a daughter's father," I manage. He takes the bottle and drinks; some leaks out of his mouth, into the dried blood on his neck.

"Thank you, brother," he says, handing it back. "I am you."

My eyes are suddenly blinded and I am spinning; it is all I can do to hand the bottle to Dora quickly and move out of the way, to the side of the road. I stumble over a hump of grass and fall on my knees.

Deeper and deeper, the sobs rise on their own and I

have to fight to breathe between them; they come from below my stomach, wracking and shaking me as if I am vomiting grief. I hear a moan, wailing out of control, and I realize it is me.

Once, when my eyes open briefly, I glimpse the marchers' legs passing by, dust rising around them. I lie down on my side, facing them, still heaving, hearing a softer version of the moaning sound.

*Emma was the love of my life.*

*Oh, not in the way that sounds. Although that was what I had feared for so long.*

*For as long as I can remember, I felt I was supposed to have a sister. I treasured my baby brother, my closest friend, but always waited for her to come, too. When I learned, at five, that my mother had lost a baby, I was sure it was my missing sister.*

*In my dreams or reveries, she appeared as a redhead. There were none in my family, on either side, as far back as we knew. But my sister, the one I waited for, had red hair.*

*And then, in the hospital, the tiny child in my arms smiled up at me, her face framed in thin but distinctly copper-red hair.*

*As a child, I loved the song "Scarlet Ribbons," and always cried at the end:*

*"If I live to be a hundred,*

*I will never know from where*

*Came those lovely scarlet ribbons,*

*Scarlet ribbons for her hair."*

*That verse came to me again as I held newborn Emma. Where did her ribbons of red hair come from?*

*And she herself?*

*I felt as if the first day of Creation was at hand, and I had watched as God set out the galaxies and then handed me a burning, newmade star and said —*

*"Take care of this one."*


Kneeling now in the dust, I feel I've failed.

I'd known before she was born that Emma's life was to be about her — not about me, or her mother, or her family.

I'd lived my whole young life with the pressure of the past, feeling myself — my ability to make choices — warped and overwhelmed by all those who came before me, what they sacrificed, what they expected. And I'd watched Phoebe's passion and talent for art be slowly, relentlessly crushed by a family heritage of poverty, fear, and addiction.

I knew the most important thing we could do for our children would be to free them from our unlived lives, and those of our parents and grandparents before us. To quiet those nagging ancestral cries, so each child could hear the still, small voice within — and follow wherever it led.

I knew that. I knew it with every fiber of my being. And yet ... here I am in the dust, having to admit that from the day she was born, my love for Emma has not simply been for Emma. It's been colored, stained, maybe ruined, by selfishness — by what she meant to me. My need for that missing sister, for someone to heal the loneliness I didn't know I felt.

*I'd been given a priceless gift, a divine seed to tend, to water and weed as it grew. But how much of the time had I spent looking raptly not at that precious plant, but at its image in my mind ...*

*Like those countless fathers who are never home, always away "at work," who fondly show strangers tiny photographs of the children they aren't with ...*

*I'm not merely like them — I'm one of them. My wallet photos are years out of date, and I see the photos more often than I see the real children.*

*Maybe that's how we all are, how we all fail. Divorced or not, we fall away from the family, trying to provide. Whether we're pursuing our dreams or serving time in an office cubicle, we fathers wander — or are driven — farther and farther from the heart of the home ...*

*And maybe our love for a child is always <u>our</u> love, always comes through the person we are.*

*Maybe love can't come any other way. Maybe it must always be colored — saturated, even — by the all-too-human vessel it pours through.*

*It all feels so hopeless ...*


When the storm of grief has at last subsided, and I can breathe without gasping, I wipe my eyes and nose and look.

The road is empty. Two legs stand before me: Dora. She offers a handkerchief.

"Thank you," I say, taking it, "but this is not right." Trying to speak makes my breath ragged; my voice trembles and breaks. "I should be alone. You should not have to take care of me."

"I do not have to," she says gently, taking hold of my arm. "I choose to."

She hands me the water bottle.

"And you will be alone soon enough."

♦ ♦ ♦

At last, just before sunset, we reach Oyster Village. More people meet us outside town, hurling their broken objects, scattering the dogs, who are afraid to enter the town. By now, all of us are helping the weary dancers pick up broken things and put them into the bags.

A tall, commanding woman with steel-grey hair leads us to a fenced yard where the grey dancers leave the bags, chanting a song in a call-and-response mode.

Dora explains that the pottery shards will be soaked in barrels to make new clay. The broken wood will be sorted, some to be used in making new tools and utensils, some to be used as kindling.

"Nothing is wasted," she says. "Everything is used up or made new. That is what the singers are saying."

"But they are not speaking just about clay and wood, are they?" I guess.

She nods, smiling.

"Everything," she says.

Soon after, we've all had a long drink, or many, and rinsed our hands and faces at a fountain. On it, carved grey stone orcas and whales dance. The villagers invite us to join them in gathering around the dancers in the square, as we did at Owl Village. The musicians begin, the dancing resumes. This time, the scenes are brief.

Breaker and Little Mother enter; she is still wearing the red-gold circlet. His mask now carries a white beard; red ribbons cover his eyes. The two of them sit under a tree.

Then she rises and dances with a series of male dancers, all in white; one by one, they arrive and leave. Child dancers, also in white, dance with her, then leave.

"She tells him," Dora says, "that she has given her life — her suitors, her husband, her children — for his."

Three more dancers appear, one female, two males, in colored robes.

"His other children," Dora whispers.

With Little Mother, they kneel before Breaker, who is still seated under the tree. He lifts up his right hand, then brings it down violently beside a male dancer's head; he does the same to the other male dancer. Both fall and roll away.

Little Mother and the other female dancer run to tend to the fallen brothers; meanwhile, old Breaker rises and turns, walking into darkness, as the music recalls the sea and the cry of gulls.

"He walked into the sea to die?" I ask.

"Yes," says Dora.

The sun has touched the western mountains when the last scene begins.

Little Mother and her sister lead the two brothers onto the central platform and lay them down gently, as the drums beat in unison, slowly, steadily. Little Mother then embraces her sister and they dance, a last time. Then she sends her away. The sister leaves haltingly, looking back.

Once she is alone, Little Mother reaches up and removes her circlet, then extends her body to its full length, holding the circlet up into the sky as it flames with the sunset's reflected colors.

A flute cries, piercingly, and she falls atop her brothers. While the drums beat softly, the grey dancers gather around the fallen ones, then lift them and carry them off.

In the silence, an owl calls.

◆　◆　◆

It is morning. Dora and I stand at the docks. She has found a man, a fisherman, who is willing to let me take a small wooden canoe across to Bear Island.

"My daughters are there," the fisherman says, smiling, showing a bright gold tooth. "At the Women's Lodge. They will bring it back."

For the third time, he refuses payment.

"Thank you, brother," I say. His eyes widen slightly.

"Go well, brother," he says.

I put my pack into the canoe and say farewell to Dora with a hug. She agrees to take my thanks again to her grandfather, and asks me to greet Emma for her.

A seagull cries.

With the momentum of my climbing in, and a push from Dora, the boat slips off the gravelly beach and into the water.

103

*Chapter 5*

## BEAR ISLAND

Out on the open water, in the still morning, the cold moves easily through the canoe's thin wood and my thin clothes. Only steady rowing keeps me warm.

Daylight fills the air, reflecting off the thin grey cloud cover; but the sun itself has not yet appeared, has not cleared the mountains ahead of me. Looking back, I watch its gold light just touching the rocky peaks above Oyster Bay.

I keep rowing, moving slowly forward into the last shades of night, toward the deep, dark shadow of Bear Island.

*"She has given her life for his."*

*I still hear Dora's voice.*

*I still see the ghostly white suitors, the children that Breaker's daughter never had ... they seem to dance in the air before me, above the waves.*

*That was what I feared, that Emma's life might be swallowed up by mine.*

*I saw, as the divorce broke our family apart, that she'd be pressured to become the "Little Mother" for her two younger siblings. But at least, I thought, I wouldn't be leaning on her emotionally.*

*So I thought.*

*But how much, in those years, did I — did we all — rely on her precocious understanding, her maturity, her fierce love for Carlie and Tim? And her dedication to her mother?*

*How much did I rely on her love for me?*

*And didn't my leaving — looking for what I'd hoped would be a place of strength, so I could be a stronger support — didn't that leave her feeling abandoned, less safe, less loved?*

*I didn't dare ask what it cost her, not for years.*

*When she was 17, she told me.*

*"I've never had a father," she wrote.*

*I knew it was her anger speaking, wiping out the first seven years of her life, as well as the seven years I'd stayed nearby after that. But her words lacerated me.*

*"You were never there when I needed you," she said. "So I've learned to get along without one."*

*My mind protested: I'd only been gone from Phoenix three years. And I could recognize Phoebe's voice, her argument that if I loved them, I should give up my life to make money for them.*

*But I could also hear the voice of a girl who'd been overwhelmed, pushed into an adult role.*

*Beneath Emma's anger, I knew, was her pain. Her hurt and confusion at being so suddenly and inexplicably left, abandoned by the father she had loved and trusted all her life.*

*Leaving her with an impossible responsibility, two younger children and an ill mother.*

*Emma was so hurt, and I had caused it ...*

*When she sent that letter, I was living in the attic of a friend's mountain cabin. Every morning, on the winding road to work, I had to fight not to let go of the wheel and let the car plunge off into the canyon.*

*Every night, driving home, that struggle resumed. At times, exhausted by grief, I was afraid I'd lose ... so I'd pull over onto the shoulder and sleep.*

◆ ◆ ◆

Halfway across the channel, a delicate mist begins falling, so thin that it just softens the outlines of things.

I take out Althea's wool scarf, unroll it and wrap it around my neck, tucking it over my chest, glad for its instant warmth.

Soon, the droplets are large enough that I can see them hitting the placid, lightly wrinkled water. Then I can hear them; then they become a steady rain, and dark clouds blot out the bright sky. The air grows so filled with slanting rain and mist that the islands disappear.

I pull up my jacket's hood and keep rowing. There's nothing to take my bearings by.

I keep rowing. There is only the rain's drumming, and an occasional gull cry.

Then I hear — or feel, rumbling up through the boat's body — a deep vibration. My heart races, and a chill runs through me:

*What if this is a ship? I'm in an open sea lane, and I can only see thirty yards in any direction... Will I be able to avoid a freighter, or even a ferry, bearing down on me in this fog?*

I'm sitting up tense and alert, still rowing. I strain to see, and listen so intently I forget to breathe. The faint hum grows stronger, but I still can't tell what direction it's from.

All at once, just off to my left, the water pushes hard on the canoe and a black shape appears, lifting out of the sea — dark, massive and glistening, it curves and rises, ever larger and larger, then I see white — *orca!*

As slowly and gracefully as if time has stopped, this enormous being, many times larger than my small craft, bursts into air with a soft explosion of sound and steamy spray, exhaling. For a long, impossible moment, it hangs half in air, half in water. Then it slides back down, its multi-ton bulk slicing soundlessly into the closing sea. One large soft fin curves over its back like a jaunty hand salute.

Mesmerized, I forget to row. I sit, I watch. My own breath has exploded in a single gasp of awe.

One by one, a whole family — a pod — of these impossible creatures, lifts and soars and drops back into the water again and again, crossing my vision from left to right. One after another, they dance, they play, they seem to smile and laugh.

Yet all the while they are hunting. Swift, and silent, so massive, so implacable — they take what prey they choose instantly, and meet no resistance.

Nothing can flee them, nothing can impede them, these carnivorous dancing masters of the sea and air. They leap and turn, rise and fall, in a serene yet joyful progress toward wherever they desire to go, wherever ocean calls them.

Then all at once, they are gone.

Only their wake waves remain, slapping lightly on the side of my boat, jostling me again and again from my secure perch, testimony to what has visited.

*If I were a first fisherman, millennia ago, exploring this new sea for my people, would I dare to tell them of this? What could I possibly say?*

I think of Daniel the prophet in the Bible, babbling wildly about fiery wheels. I feel what must have been his hopeless hope in trying to speak the unspeakable.

It takes me many moments to gather myself, to breathe regularly again. At last, I take my oar in hand and begin to guess, from the wave patterns, where my direction lies.

♦ ♦ ♦

*I'd wake up on the car seat, aching and sore, yet relieved simply to be alive. After stretching and yawning, I'd drive on home.*

*Gradually, the desperate struggle inside me relaxed. I began to see that the pain, while great, would not kill me.*

"Perhaps what you're seeing," said Ben, the therapist I'd been consulting, "is that <u>you</u> won't kill you. That as much as it hurts to receive such a letter, there's a limit to what you'll do just to avoid feeling the pain."

*That was a surprising thought. It took me a while to absorb.*

"Well," I said at last. "The deepest pain is that I can't be a father — the father my children want, the one I want to be. And that it hurts them. But if I don't die ... then, I guess I'm still a father ... of some kind."

"Indeed," Ben said, tapping his pen. "And what might that father do?"

"Survive? Bear the pain. Theirs and mine... Take responsibility for it."

"That's a tall order," Ben said. "But it's an important way to let them know they matter to you — and that they don't have to protect you."

"Oh god," I broke in. "Like the plastic pool when they were small, letting them be angry at me. That's still my job, isn't it?"

"Part of it, yes. One thing, though."

"Yes?"

"Taking on responsibility doesn't mean accepting blame."

"Huh? But I don't want to dodge their anger, or defend myself —"

"No, no, of course not. I'm thinking of you accepting

*their present feelings, but not getting caught up in a blaming story. You see, blame looks only at the past, which none of us can change. But responsibility is about the present and the future, where we can act."*

*He'd been writing quickly on his pad, and he turned it around for me to see.*

*"Response - ability," I read.*

*"The ability to respond," he said. "Now, tomorrow, next year."*

*I laughed.*

*"Can't do that if I'm dead, can I?"*

*It felt good to be able to laugh.*

*So now, out here on this cold bit of ocean, shrouded in foggy rain, do I have some more of my job to do?*

*More accepting, being "response-able"?*

*For more than twenty years, I've been afraid of the unexpected bond with Em. I've distrusted it.*

*Can I just accept it?*

*Surely it's good for a father to feel a powerful and nurturing connection to his child. I'd always expected to feel that — a soul-deep commitment to my children. And I certainly did, instantly, without even thinking, when Matt stood in our sunroom unpacking his paper bag.*

*When Emma was born, I was given an even more intense dose of that feeling, stronger than I expected ... And?*

*And it revealed to me a sense of loneliness I hadn't*

*known I felt.*

*So?*

*So it was what it was.*

*And because it reached so deeply into a part of myself I hadn't been conscious of, I was wary. I sensed the danger of letting my unconscious needs — whatever they might be — shape or overshadow my caring for this child ...*

*That feeling arose in the man and father I was, the only one I could be, at that time. It was one of the givens — like her red hair, her incomplete upper lip, or my wide shoulders, my incomplete maturing. Givens that we'd both had to live with, from that moment forward.*

*In the years that followed, did I rely on my daughter to satisfy my unmet emotional needs, like Breaker swallowing up Little Mother's life?*

*No.*

*At least, I don't think so. For better or for worse, I continued to seek whatever I needed from the women in my life — from Phoebe, from my close women friends. And after the divorce, from my next partner ... and the partner after that.*

*The one time I had actually felt myself starting to depend on Emma, that afternoon on the driveway, it had been like tasting poison. I spit it out, resolved not to let it happen.*

*Suddenly, out here on the water, I remember a moment I'd forgotten.*

111

*Emma was 13, telling her grandmother and me the good news at brunch: She'd been accepted at the "fast-track" high school she'd chosen, one that guaranteed its graduates entrance to colleges around the world.*

*"Wonderful," my mother said. "Does that mean you're already thinking about college, too?"*

*"Not 'thinking about,' Grandma," Em said. "I've decided. I'm going to NYU."*

*"New York University!" I exclaimed. "That's a great school! But —" I thought of how fully she'd committed herself to helping to raise Tim and Carlie, and to caring for Phoebe in her bad times "—isn't it awfully far? Three thousand miles?"*

*"Dad," she said with an indulgent laugh, raising her iced tea glass, "when I'm 18, I'm gettin' the hell outta Dodge!"*

*She was as good as her word. The afternoon she received her diploma, she also had won a full scholarship. She moved to Manhattan in the fall.*

*I don't use Emma now, don't burden her as my confidante, don't ask that she understand all I'm going through. I know how that, too, can land with unbearable weight on a child.*

*But if I know what not to do, I'm not sure what to do. I may be too careful, I think; I don't stay in touch enough. I don't know any more how to share our lives; I fear burdening her with unwanted details of mine, or intruding into hers.*

*She doesn't complain. Would she? I don't know.*

*Is this the best I can do at being a father right now? If it is, can I accept it?*

*If it isn't, I want to do better — if I can just figure
out what better is.*

♦ ♦ ♦

Eventually, the fog clears and I can make out a small,
shell-littered beach ahead. Pulling the canoe up onto it,
I'm grateful that the rain has stopped and the warm sun
is drying out my soaked clothes.

But I'm also concerned. In the rain, I seem to have
wandered to the south. I can see I'm now below Bear
Island's west-protruding arm, instead above it.

But I'm too tired to paddle back around it. So I'm
landing in a place where no one expects to see a visitor,
and I'll have to work my way overland to find the
village.

I tie the canoe to a weathered web of roots well above
the tide line. Shouldering my pack, I realize I have no
food — won't be eating until I find the village. But I do
have water.

I scan the beach for a creek running out to the sea.
Seeing none, I head into the trees and up the forested
hillside, in as northerly a line as I can manage.

When I reach the crest, I see that there's at least one
more ridge between me and the harbor. It's warm,
midday. I take a sip from the water bottle, and start
down into the ravine between this ridge and the next.

Soon I'm struggling steeply downhill through the
underbrush, which looks soft and beautiful with ferns
and mosses under the tall old trees. But it's also heavy
going, littered with fallen trunks and branches,

overgrown with blackberries and other vines.

After perhaps half an hour, I reach a creek at the bottom. Its gentle voice, and the cool green shade, are too good to pass by. I sit on a flat rock above a pool, set down my pack, and take off my shoes.

My feet slip gratefully into the cold water. Large water spiders, as thin as if they're made of web silk, skate away, light as lace on the stream's surface.

Beneath them, I notice nymphs — we called them "hellgramites" in my youth, as we peered into similar streams in redwood forests. Like hermit crabs, they crawl along, hidden under long, cone-shaped turbans they fashion from shells, tiny pebbles, mica chips, and other stream-bottom debris.

In a quick movement, betrayed by bright spots of orange, a crawfish steps out from under a rock, searching. It waits, its feathery gills fluttering with eager breath; then it is gone.

Minnows dart like whispering tongues between rock and rock. A clutch of trout fingerlings ride the current together, facing upstream.


*Mistakes.*

*I made a mistake in the fog, took the wrong direction. Now I'm here, working my way toward where I'm supposed to be. I've got a day's work more than I expected, making up for that error.*

*But I can do it. I enjoy the challenge, even. And it's beautiful — a privilege just to be here, really. In this calm, green world full of lovely creatures and surprises ...*

*Is this how it is for Emma?*

*Have my mistakes — in the fog of unknowing — given her a longer road to travel, mountains to work her way across?*

*And does she grow stronger, more confident from handling all the challenges? Even as she feels anger, justified anger, and deep hurt beneath it? Is she also able to be refreshed by the beauty along the way?*

*I think of that Navajo blessing way prayer:*

*"I walk in beauty.*

*Beauty before me,*

*beauty behind me,*

*beauty above me,*

*beauty below me.*

*Beauty all around me.*

*It is finished in beauty."*

*That's how I want it to be for Emma — and for each of my children. Whatever obstacles I've put in their path, I pray I can help them find — and walk in — the beauty.*

Something moves noisily in the underbrush. I turn to look, and a jay loudly warns the woods of a presence — mine, or whoever is moving in the brush.

Reluctantly, I admit that it is time.

Slipping my feet out of the water, I thank the creek's pond dwellers for sharing their comforting, cool world. I step across the creek, put on my socks and shoes, and begin climbing upward.

By the time I reach the top of the second ridge, the sun has slid well down the sky. I'm tired and a little hungry, and relieved that my journey has been a success. Yet I'm almost sad to see the beach and small harbor after a slow, silent day alone.

Halfway down the slope to the sea, I come across a well-maintained path. I follow it off to the right, northeast, hoping it curves around the beach and toward the village. It does.

With a half-hour's easy walking, I arrive at the village. A small cluster of buildings set behind a pair of docks, one long, one short. It is late afternoon.

"Women's Lodge?" repeats the man sitting in the weathered, unpainted shed that serves as a boat and bait shop. He is weathered himself, though about my age, and he is carefully planing a board of white pine. "Easy to find," he says, "but not so easy to get into. At least not for you and me."

He smiles. A large black cat, reposing on a shelf behind him, lifts its head and yawns as if joining in the joke.


Following his directions, I take a main path that seems to head east. The land lifts off the beach gently into wooded glades and hills. I can see the steep ridge I came down behind me, and a higher range of mountains up ahead.

Level sunset light throws long, soft beams through the thick boughs, illuminating galaxies of dust. There is glare in the light and a soft darkness in the shadows. I hear insects singing.

I've walked less than a mile when I come to a fallen log across the path. I step over it.

"Hold," a voice says calmly, from the dusk among the trees to my right. "Wait."

I hear a rustling in the brush to my left, behind a large old double-trunk cedar. But no one emerges.

I stand and listen to the insects humming, birds peeping and twittering. I'm tempted to walk on. But something tells me to relax, so I sit on the log.

"Good," says another voice, from behind the big cedar. "Why are you here?"

"I am looking for the Women's Lodge," I say.

"For what purpose?" the first voice asks, sharply.

"I have a message for Ania and Kamoa, from their father in Oyster Bay."

"Yes?" from the cedar.

"He has loaned me his canoe, and it is tied up on a beach south of here, across those ridges." I point to the way I've come. "I promised him I would tell them, so they can take it home."

"They will have your message."

"I also want to thank them."

"Consider it done."

I stand a moment, silent.

"And then?" asks the voice on the right, as it draws nearer.

"I do not know. My daughter told me to come here."

"Ah."

Branches move on my right, and a figure steps partly out of the trees, just visible in the dusky half-light. A tall woman with a mantle of long, loose hair.

"You are expected. Go on until you come to a rock garden, then walk up the hill to your right. Your place will be there."

"Thank you," I say, rising.

There is no answer but insects and birdsong.

On a small knoll above the rock garden, maybe thirty yards from the path, I find a shed sided in rough cedar. It has a small dirt porch before it, under a light wooden awning.

A chair and table are there, and on the table is an evening meal. In a covered bowl, a steaming porridge of beans and rice, carrots and onions; on a plate covered by a napkin held down by pebbles at its corners, two thick slabs of sourdough bread and two strips of dried salmon. A second bowl holds a fresh salad; a ceramic pitcher, glazed pale green with streaked, half-hidden droplets of bright red, holds cold, cold water.

I am tired and grateful, not having eaten all day. But I know that if I am to make this meal last, I must slow myself. In the shed, I sit on the bed and take off my shoes and socks. My feet stretch happily, and I decide to take off all my clothes, getting the pitcher and using a few handfuls of water to rinse myself off behind the shed. It seems no one is watching.

A large towel hangs on the bathroom door; I dry myself and tie it around my waist. Putting Althea's scarf over my shoulders, I go out to the table. I sit, quietly, breathing deep and letting my day's journey come fully to an end. I sip some of the wonderful water and breathe, watching the beams of sunlight lift upward and disappear, as the sun slides away and evening begins.

I eat my meal in quiet, alone, serenaded by the busy twilight singing and chittering of birds and squirrels, chipmunks, foxes, whoever is gathering food or children before the night.

"Vespers," I think, as the last gentle energy of the forest's day dies down, and silence descends with darkness.

*The thought of vespers takes me back to the time when Carlie was born, when our family's life was wrapped in a worshipping community and morning and evening prayer shaped our days. We brought Carlie home from the hospital to a little bungalow in a neighborhood by the lake, where birds and insects sang the sun to sleep.*

*Sleep — ha!*

*Suddenly I'm in that dining room, moonlight winking off the beveled glass of the built-in oak cabinets ... I'm walking around and around the long table, talking and singing and keeping up a steady rhythm of firm, gentle pats on the back of the tiny form curled into my shoulder.*

*Carlie has colic, can't sleep, cries ... and so each night becomes father-daughter time, as we make our circuits of the dining room, hour after hour, while the rest of the family sleeps.*

*At first, I'm a bit reluctant, since I have to be up in the morning for work. But soon this becomes a magic time, and though I get teased at the office about "diaper bags" under my eyes, I look forward to carrying Carlie on our long night travels in search of the lost land of sleep.*

To my surprise, a colony of lightning bugs begins dancing into the air, twinkling, from near the rock garden; they are smaller, more silvery, than the big golden ones I have known. I sit, tilting my stout chair back against the shed, until stars start to peek between the tall, dark trees.

Then I hear voices, talking on the road. I step into the cabin and slip on my jeans and jacket; as I zip the jacket, my hand brushes the snake skull on my chest and I smile.

"Hello, Sister," I murmur, laying a finger on it.

Just then, the door swings open.

"Hi, Dad."

There, holding a lantern, is a slender young woman with light auburn hair pulled back and braided behind her calm, quick-eyed face — Carlie. For a long moment, we look quietly at each other; it is so good to see her, it warms me and makes me smile.

"You need to stay here tonight," she says. "All night. And not go out. I'll be at the Lodge."

"Alright," I say.

"I'll come get you in the morning," she says. "Be ready for some hiking."

"Some *more* hiking," I say, with a rueful grin.

"Yes," she says. "I've got to go now."

She turns, and walks back toward the path. I'm surprised at how she has grown, taller now than a year ago — but moving with the same easy, fluid power she's always had. The athlete, the actor, the adventurer — the child with all the broken bones.

"See you in the morning," I call softly. Just when I

think she has not heard, the lantern lifts and falls, waving.

My body feels tired enough to sleep, but seeing Carlie has banished rest for a while. On the porch, I discover a bucket of hot water left for me to wash in. Since I've already rinsed off, I use it to wash my clothes, hanging them on the nearest low branches to dry.

As I wash I am thinking, remembering ...

*We're in a tiny desert cabin that friends have given us to use while we visit Phoebe's family.*

*Phoebe, hugely pregnant with Timmy, is catching a nap in the bedroom. Matt has taken Em out to look for lizards; I'm writing, keeping an eye on Carlie. Carlie's hard at work, earnestly tottering along beside the couch and coffee table, holding on with one hand, on the verge of walking.*

*The phone interrupts and I grab it, before it wakes Phoebe. Out of the corner of my eye, I see Carlie climb up onto the couch.*

*"Ah, good," I think. "She'll rest a while."*

*When I finish the short phone conversation, I look to see if Carlie's falling asleep. Instead, I see her standing on the back of the couch — how she climbed up there, I can't guess — one hand pressing on the wall. She starts to step, lets go, wavers — and before I can rush to catch her, she has caught her balance. Confidently, arms out, she then walks the entire length of the couch, teetering on its back.*

*When I gather her in my arms to congratulate her, I wonder if the others will believe me when I tell them.*

*But of course, they do — it's Carlie.*

*Weeks later, I'm sitting with our friends on the edge of their huge pool, at the shallow end, talking.*

*Matt is jumping off the diving board, Emma is wading near us with water wings. Carlie is across the pool, standing on a stair, the water almost up to her diaper.*

*Suddenly, too quickly for thought, something tells my body what her body has in mind — in mid-sentence, I realize I'm no longer talking but underwater, on a long dive. It ends right where Carlie is toppling in.*

*Instantly, we're bursting up out of the water, splashing and breathing, her small surprised body aloft in my hands.*

*I never stop being grateful for whatever took over my mind and body in that moment ...*

Voices interrupt my remembering.

Many voices, chanting.

I hang my underwear over a shrub and walk a little way up the rise past the shed. From here, I can see a bright glow between the trees where the Lodge must be.

The women are singing, beginning a ceremony. I can hear the shape of a melody, but can't make out any words.

I stand for a while listening, leaning back against a young fir tree. I wonder what Carlie is doing, what they're all doing. I step onward, aimlessly, quietly.

Then twigs snap — off to my right — and I stop, frozen, holding my breath.

In the corner of my eye, a golden body emerges from the low boughs. Silently, I exhale and do not move.

The deer steps forward — a stag, with six or eight points on his magnificent antlers. He moves toward the light, ears up as if listening to the voices. Slowly, he takes a step, and then another, another...

*Hello, brother*, I think. *Thank you for showing yourself.*

Then a dog voice barks out; the stag turns, quick as the flick of a hand, and is gone, back into the forest.

*We males are not supposed to be here,* I say to his vanished form. *This is not our place.*

I stand a moment, letting go of the muffled songs, then walk back to the shed to get ready for bed.

Stepping into my dark room, I hear a whisper of sound. A small lizard skitters out the door and away, into the grass. I slip into bed and am asleep before I know it.


*We're in the car together, the younger three children and I, on one of our visitation weekends.*

*It's Carlie's turn to "ride shotgun" — sit beside me; Timmy and Emma sit in back. I'm talking in the voice of a leprechaun we made up years ago. Emma, now ten or eleven, declares that she doesn't want to hear it — she's bored with "McMac."*

*But Carlie and Tim both chant all five of his names, forcing him to appear. They fire questions at him, trying to trick him into telling where his treasure is.*

*Suddenly, picking up on Em's attitude, Carlie gets a wicked gleam in her eye.*

*"McMac," she asks, "d'you remember Wednesday, what happened to you on your way to school?"*

*She invents a tale of how his pants got caught on a bush, and he had to go to class in his underwear. The leprechaun sputters and denies, mortified; Carlie and Tim are shouting with delight, and even Em is giggling.*

*This starts a whole new tradition, and grants the leprechaun a few more years of life.*

The sound of knocking startles me awake.

"Morning, Dad. It's time."

Carlie hands my dry clothes through the door and I dress quickly. When I step out, pulling my pack onto my back, she hands me an apple, an orange and a bag of nuts.

"Breakfast," she says, smiling. Another person is with her: the tall woman who detained me on the path. "This is Themis. She'll be going with us part of the way. Ready?"

I nod, and we set off on the road east. As we pass the Lodge, voices and the clatter of dishes drift into the soft air. I start to ask about last night, then think better of it. So I ask instead where we'll be hiking today.

"Into the center of the island," Themis says. "There's a valley there, and a lake."

As we hike, we speak little except about the trail, which Themis finds and follows with a sure knowledge. Through the thick underbrush, she leads us deftly by a series of animal trails and natural paths.

I begin to feel that yesterday, I was blundering through the forest. I offer silent apologies for the ways I did not know to avoid breaking through its web of life.

Toward mid-morning, with the sun rising higher and the land beneath us growing steeper, the going gets fairly hard. Once again, I'm grateful for my recent months of exercise as I stretch and push to keep up with Themis. Carlie's hanging back a bit to help me along.

After a half-hour of this climbing, Themis stops. When we reach her, she indicates a mossy cedar log that has fallen long ago from somewhere nearby in the forest.

"Ready for a break?" she asks, sitting down.

"You bet," I say, gratefully finding a level spot. "Carlie, have you used this path before? You seem to know your way around."

"Actually, I haven't," she says, "but Themis is an easy guide to follow."

"You are indeed," I say to the older woman. "Thank you for setting a pace I could follow. And Carlie's always been good at finding her way. Remember in Victoria that time, when you left the museum?"

Carlie cocks her head, unsure.

"We were at the Natural History Museum —"

"With all the monkeys," she says, smiling and nodding.

*I'm standing at the entrance to the museum, where the boys voted to go when the girls voted to go shopping. All the girls but Carrie, our tomboy — and now she doesn't like the museum.*

*"It smells weird in there, Dad. It makes me feel bad ... I can't get my breath."*

*The boys have gone off without her, which has probably added to her discomfort.*

*"Can I go to the mall, where Aunt Elaine and the girls are?"*

*Her brown eyes look at me, pleading.*

*I feel with a chill that this has suddenly become a major moment. She's only eight years old; bright for her age, but ... I temporize.*

*"I can't take you there, Car'. I've got to stay with the boys."*

*She nods. Wisps of her hair, darkened from the red-blonde of infancy to auburn, blow across her face.*

*"I know where it is, Dad. I can find them once I get there."*

*This is my adventurous child, the one who took her first steps while teetering along the back of the couch. The one who learns by throwing herself in, and who has already been to the emergency room more times than the other three combined.*

*She's also whip-smart and reliable. And I know in my gut that she relies on me to let her take on challenges, to show what she can do. (Her mother is, perhaps naturally, a more protective parent.)*

*"Show me how you would go," I say. My use of a hypothetical is a feeble attempt.*

*She eagerly points out the route, including the places where she has to stop and wait for lights, watch for traffic.*

*I sigh.*

*"Good job, kiddo. Promise you'll stick to the plan? No hurrying? No side trips?"*

*"Promise." A pause, a quick breath. "Will you watch me?"*

*"Every step of the way," I say.*

*We hug, she starts off — and I realize she is carrying my heart. I want to cry out, to call her back. I think of the boys — they'll need some supervision pretty soon, but I can't take my eyes off that small form moving among all those people and cars and busses.*

*It's the longest ten minutes of my life. Carrie makes every step, just as she planned; at the corners, she turns back and waves.*

*Then she disappears around the corner of the block where the mall is ... and the longest ten minutes becomes the longest two hours.*

*When we finally meet up with the girls for lunch, and she's with them, I take my first real breath.*

"Are you ready for more?" Themis asks.

"Right." I stand up and stretch out, hearing a welcome crack in my back. "Lay on, Macduff."

We spend another hour climbing up the steady incline. Then we have to walk along the broad back of a gigantic fallen trunk, grabbing onto its now upright branches to hold ourselves steady. At the end, we reach a wide granite boulder where the huge tree hit as it fell, snapping its top off. Carlie stops and points. I peer out, and down, and see the broken top dozens of feet below us, on a wide ledge; beneath it drops a dizzying precipice, perhaps two hundred feet down to the tops

127

of ancient trees.

"Wow," I exhale, panting.

"Surprising, huh?" Carlie laughs. She nods at a vast bowl ringed by mountains that spreads out before us. "There's the lake."

In the bowl, surrounded by forest, lies a wide oval of pale green meadow. In its center, it seems a gem-blue piece of sky has fallen; like an open eye, the lake reflects clouds riding through it.

I cannot speak. The lake glows, pure and serene, appearing untouched in this hidden place. Framing my view, at one side, is Carlie's profile. The water seems to mirror not simply her beauty, but her deep, crystalline purity of soul. All the morning's effort has won this moment, this meeting with a mystery.

"It's important that you see this lake," Themis says, "and know its story.

"Ages and ages ago, before we were people on the Earth, when the mountains and islands were still forming themselves, other beings we might call gods or spirits walked here. They still do — but with their human children everywhere now, the Older Ones take care not to be seen or heard, except when they wish to be.

"One such being is the one my people call Quail Goddess, a daughter of the All-Maker. Do you know the sound of a quail flying?"

"Yes," I said. "A sudden whirring sound—"

"Sudden because they take off from the grass cover before you even know they're there," Carlie adds.

"Just so," says Themis, "and like well-made, well-shot arrows, they fly swift and straight and low. Quail

Goddess is an archer. A hunter. The forest belongs to her, and all beings in it are under her care.

"When their time here is done, it is her swift, sure arrow that finds them. And she is also the one who watches over young lives — she leads each newborn out of the mother's womb and into the world. Youth and innocence are in her special care."

Themis sweeps her hand toward the lake.

"There, in that lake, is where she bathes each evening to renew her immortal life. It is a sacred, secret place. No one may visit near sunset, or before sunrise, when she is there.

"But once, someone did. You know the story of the Great War at Many Smokes."

"Yes," I say, "I have been learning of it."

"After that war, among those who came home was a young man of this island we called Track. He won this name because he — and his dogs — had learned to find and follow the tracks of many of the creatures we live among, to find them in their hidden places. Track was not a killer, not a fighter, but when the war came, he went. And when he came back, he was not as young as when he had left. Not only was he years older from the long, long war — his soul had been aged, and not at all gently, by what he experienced there. He found it hard to be among us, because the worst of the war still lived in him, and would erupt at unexpected moments.

"Eventually, he took his dogs, whom he loved, and went to dwell alone in the forest. He remained available to us when we needed his skills, but he lived in solitude. The war dreams, with their horrible feeling of being real, still came upon him; but now, he could weather them like a storm, and not fear hurting anyone else.

"Track had lived this way for a few years when he was out one night, walking off a dream, with his dogs. Following some small-animal track they had found — a badger perhaps, or a beaver — they came upon this lake. It was just before sunrise, when the night's darkness begins to separate into shadows, and only shapes and movement can be seen.

"Track's eye was caught by something moving, something that seemed to be in the middle of the lake. His dogs saw it, too. Wondering what this could possibly be, he held his gaze, intending to see it better as the sun rose. But suddenly, a last beam from the setting moon shot over the trees — perhaps a cloud had moved — and there, standing on the water's surface, at the deepest part of the lake, was the form of a woman. She was radiant, the most beautiful being he had ever seen, and he could only stare as she bent to cup water and then poured it over herself.

"He knew she could not be human, standing on the water like that, and as his stunned mind realized who she must be, he involuntarily breathed her name: 'Quail Goddess!' And one of his dogs let out a short, low whine.

"She turned to look, and at once, as her eyes met his, he could feel himself beginning to heal, changing deep within, below his heart. Again, without any thought, he stepped forward, raising his arm — and he heard a sudden whirring sound, and felt the air as something flew past his ear. He turned, but could not see what it had been; and when he turned back, he knew. She was just lowering her bow. Where it had come from, he could not begin to guess before she spoke.

"'Mortal,' she said. 'You have followed me here.'"

"'No, goddess,' he stammered. 'I did not know—'"

"'And you have gazed upon me in my nakedness.'"

"'Yes, I see you are, but I—'"

"'And you want...?'"

"'Nothing, goddess, but to thank you.'"

"'Thank me?'"

"'For what you have given me. Somehow, when you looked into my eyes, this terrible war that I have been carrying inside me turned at last to a peace. I — I can never—'"

"'Ah,' said the goddess. 'I understand. This is good. But you, too, must understand. This is my sacred place, my sacred time, and there is a price any mortal must pay for seeing me thus.'"

"'A price? Goddess, I have little, I live alone, but what I have ...'"

"'That price is death. But because you came in innocence, and have not violated my sanctuary with any earthly desires, I offer you this. Kneel, mortal.'"

Track knelt, his knees trembling, and his dogs knelt with him. He heard a soft music, as though breathed through a reed flute, and felt that change that had begun in him continue ... until he could feel his flesh contracting, and his form growing smaller ... until he and his dogs had become something else entirely — flowers at the edge of the water, their blue petals bowing toward the center of the lake.

"If you could go there," Themis says, "you would see them still. The flowers' descendants ring the lake, standing at its edge, heads bowed toward the center."

"But I will not?" I ask.

"No," she says. "That is reserved for those of the Women's Lodge."

Carlie nods, quietly. "I will be among them tomorrow."

"Today," Themis says, rising, "she will take you where you must go next." Themis then bids us farewell, and begins retracing the difficult route we have taken, back to the lodge.

When she has disappeared down the long tree trunk, into the green, Carlie turns and points toward the lake.

Three hawks are circling in the air before us, high above the treetops, the wide loops of their flight barely overlapping. Eventually, one drops toward the meadow, swift as one of Quail Goddess's arrows. Its cry, muffled by distance, reaches us after it has already disappeared toward its prey. The other two continue their calm, rhythmic circling, the delicate fingertips of their wings testing each breath of air they ride on.

*I'm on the freeway in a friend's sports car, pushing 100 miles an hour, weaving through the traffic, hoping a policeman will notice — I'd like an escort to make this safer. I don't slow down. Once I'm off the freeway, I race down the middle of the widest streets, lights flashing, horn blowing.*

*When I drive up onto the grass at the school, there is Carlie's body on a stretcher next to the high-jump pit. She calls out when she sees me, and starts to cry; she can't feel anything below her neck.*

*I hold her hand and talk to her, brushing her damp hair and kissing her eyes and face, until they lift her into the helicopter. It can't carry my weight, too, the pilot says — she must fly alone. We both cry as she rises into the air, and I shout "I love you!" into a deafening noise ...*

*Two years later, we are dancing, Carlie in a ruffled pink dress with crinolines, me in jeans and a leather jacket. A rock-and-roll love song from thirty years ago is playing on the loudspeakers. Dozens of similar couples dance beneath the crepe paper in the gym. The men are tall, leaving their youth behind; the girls are shorter (most of them), and are just entering theirs.*

*Carlie and I are trying to hold onto a rose, but in the jitterbug contest we lose it. Then Carlie is one of the finalists in a hula hoop contest, and after she is done, we find the rose lying on the floor. We rinse it off in the water fountain.*

*On the way home, we stop for ice cream ...*

Carlie's hand settles on my shoulder.

"It's another hour," she says. "Maybe longer. Do you want to rest, or go on?"

"I want to stay here forever," I say. "But give me a minute, and then let's go. I'll never forget this."

I reach around behind me and unhook the water bottle. We each take a drink. A draft of cool air sweeps over us slowly, then the forest's warm tangy scent returns.

She hands the water bottle back.

"Let's go," she says. She steps to the right edge of the boulder and jumps onto the needle-matted soil. After a minute or two walking on the ridge, we start to descend.

It takes just about an hour through the cool, shaded forest to reach a narrow valley with a creek running along its far edge.

"Lunch?" Carlie asks.

"Wonderful," I say. The hike down from the ridgetop has sharpened my appetite.

She props her pack against a log and spreads a small square of cloth on its back, where bark has fallen off to reveal countless maze-like paths cut by tiny borer beetles. She sets down two eggs, a pair of hard sweet oat cakes, two carrots and a small jar holding chunks of green. I laugh to see the green.

"You still love it?"

"Still do," she says, twisting the jar top off and offering it. Tasting the pickled broccoli, I remember how we would laugh at Carlie's tiny hand reaching past her soft baby foods for Emma's or Matt's plate. Her favorite targets were "brocky" and "spout"; Matt and Em, having more normal young palates, were happy to let her take all the broccoli and brussels sprouts she wanted.

We're peeling the shells off our eggs when she looks at me.

"You've done well, Dad," she says. "Better than I thought you would."

"Thanks," I say. I start to say more, but it's not needed. We eat quietly, enjoying the tastes and the occasional calling of the birds who live in the alpine valley.

After lunch, we cross the valley to the creek. We kneel and fill our water bottles.

"This creek goes through a fold in the mountains, over there," Carlie says, pointing east, ahead of us. "That's where you'll be going."

"You won't?" I ask.

"No. I have to head back to the Lodge. Someone will be meeting you here." She looks at the sun. "We're early, though. Thanks to your keeping up so well," she grins. "I should be able to make it well before dark."

I sigh and stand, holding out my hands. She rises, taking them in hers.

"Thank you, Carlie. This morning has been a gift, priceless."

She smiles and drops my hands.

"Good luck, Dad."

She stands a moment, we look at each other, then she turns and strides swiftly back into the forest. In moments, I have lost her among the trees.

Leaning against a knobbed old cedar, I wait, watching and listening to the creek. I sit back down to take off my shoes and drape my socks across my backpack. Now that I'm no longer moving, I can really feel the day's hiking. With a meal in my stomach, in the shady afternoon air, I am soon drowsing.

*A few years after our dance, Carlie came to live with me. She had dropped out of high school, bored — and scared by the drugs and sex her classmates were getting into.*

*I told her I agreed high school was a waste of her time.*

135

*"You can try to find what does interest you, something you really love,"* I told her, *"And you can live with me for as long as that takes.*

*"Or, if you want to get a job to make money, I'll charge you rent so you get used to budgeting, and you can live here 'til you're eighteen."*

*"I already know what I love,"* she said. *"You know, Dad — acting."*

*I laughed.*

*"Remember when you were four and Em got her first part in a play?"*

*"At KidStage,"* Carlie said.

*"You and Timmy sat through every rehearsal."*

*"And on the way home, we helped Emma say the lines."*

*"And then at Emma's next play —"*

*"The Canterville Ghost,"* she said.

*"Right. One day Alice, the director, began rehearsal by announcing that an actor had gotten sick and had to drop out."*

*"Tanya, with the long braids."*

*"Yes, and while Alice was asking us to help find a replacement, you ran up onstage —"*

*Carlie laughs, blushing.*

*"—and you started saying Tanya's lines."*

*"My first play,"* Carlie said. *"I loved it. We were in every KidStage show for years."*

*The next day, Carlie and I went to the local community college. The drama teachers welcomed*

Carlie and said she could register for class — no need for a diploma — or just join the current play's backstage crew. She grabbed the chance to work on the show, opting to wait before tackling college courses.

As we left, one instructor called to us.

"By any chance, do you act?" he asked me.

"Yes!" Carlie shouted.

"Well, I did," I said, "several years ago."

"We haven't found anyone for a small part in this show, and I wonder if you might ..."

"Thank you," I said, "but this is really my daughter's place now, and I don't want to —"

"Dad!" she cut in. "Please?"

So we did an impromptu audition.

"My first play in twenty years," I said, as we were getting in the car.

"You'll love it," she said. "Besides," she added, winking, "I'm gonna need a ride home after rehearsals."


We went out for sushi to celebrate, and the conversation took a more serious turn.

"Dad, if we're going to live together," she said, "I need to tell you something."

I paused while dipping my California roll in the wasabi and soy sauce she had mixed.

"Yes?"

"This is hard to say, but I'm really angry."

*"You are?"*

*"I've been angry a long time ... I feel — I've always felt — like you don't care about me. Like for you, Emma comes first. And I — I don't matter."*

*"Oh, Carlie," I said.*

*"No, don't say it. You always say you love me, or you love us all the same — Mom says it, too — but it's not what I feel. I feel like you're always watching what Em does, paying attention to her ... I can just disappear and you don't even notice."*

*"Carlie," I said, reaching my hands out.*

*"No," she said again. "I need to say this."*

*For several minutes — I don't know how long, but the waiter came and went silently a few times — Carlie unrolled a tale of being overlooked, unseen, even at school.*

*"It's always, 'Oh, you're Emma's sister,' and that's it — I've disappeared. Again."*

*She told of feeling lost, and hopeless, and finally realizing that it was unfair and she was mad about it.*

*"So that's why I'm telling you." She ended, with a shaky sigh. "If it makes you mad, I don't care. It's how I feel."*

*"Wow," I said, and sat quiet a minute.*

*"This must have been incredibly hard for you to say," I finally said. "I'm proud of you for having the courage to say it. And," I took a deep, shaky breath myself, "I can't imagine how hard it's been to feel this way all these years."*

*Tears started pooling in her eyes. I held out my napkin, but she shook her head and picked up her own.*

*"It breaks my heart to learn you've felt this way," I said. "I'm so sorry. I never meant — or ever wanted — for you to feel anything like it. Ever."*

*She gave a little half-nod, as if she wanted to believe me but didn't dare.*

*"I do have to tell you," I went on, "to me you are a miracle ... a gift so great I can't even put it into words."*

*She was shaking her head again.*

*"I know you probably don't believe it, and may not want to hear it right now. But this is what I have to say, what I feel ... and I hope I'll keep on telling you this as long as I live. Carlie, if I never had any other child, or any other good thing in my life, I would still thank God on my knees for letting me be — or try to be — your father."*

*We were both crying now.*

*After a while, we could breathe again.*

*"I'm not done," she said. "But I can't talk about it more right now."*

*"Okay," I said. "Please keep on telling me. If you need to say it, I need to hear it."*


*In the months that followed, Carlie did a small part (and nearly won the lead) in another play. Then auditions were announced for Laramie Project, a harrowing non-fiction study of town dealing with the murder of a gay youth.*

*It's also difficult because each actor has to create eight or ten characters. Auditions weren't open to beginning actors — a rare thing in college theatre.*

139

*"I have to do this play, Dad," Carlie said as I drove her home from class one night. "It's too ... too important." She mentioned a friend in Phoenix, and then couldn't speak.*

*"Well, you were just in Lana's acting class," I said. "Did you tell her?"*

*As soon as we got home, we began practicing. We grabbed any plays we could find, taking turns doing all the characters.*

*A week later, she marched out of her acting class wearing a broad smile.*

*"Ten o'clock Saturday," she said. "We're on the list."*

*Saturday morning, we stepped onto the long ramp leading up to the theatre's back door.*

*"Oh God," she said, clutching my arm. "All of a sudden, I'm scared."*

*"Me too," I confided. "But we're in this together."*

*On an impulse, we locked arms and danced up the ramp, singing "Off to See the Wizard."*

*For six months, Carlie was the only teenage actor in a cast of ten. At end of the run, LA's leading gay theatre invited us onto their stage, and she was acting in Hollywood.*


*Then she surprised me again.*

*One morning, Carlie arose from the friend's couch she'd slept on and borrowed a camera. She drove into a nearby wooded canyon and spent the morning snapping pictures.*

*Later, I took the film to the local camera store. I thought she'd like seeing her photos.*

*When we went for the prints, the shop owner asked who had shot them.*

*"I did," she said shyly. "This was my first time —"*

*"Young lady," he said, "please don't let it be your last. And I'm not saying this to sell film."*

*He sighed, smiling.*

*"I was thirty years a photographer with the movie studios, and now I'm twenty years here, seeing the work of thousands. You —" he fanned the prints out on the counter, "— are a natural. You have the eye. Let me show you."*

*A few months later, Carlie sat down in the kitchen one morning, coffee in hand, and asked to talk.*

*"We've been looking at me transferring to a four-year school, or going professional ..." She took a sip.*

*"Or doing both," I reminded her.*

*"Right," she said. "And I love acting. I do. But ... I've been thinking of something else, too. I got a catalog for this school in Santa Barbara ..."*

*From her backpack, she took a glossy color folder.*

*"Institute of Photography?" I read.*

*"Yes," she said. "I've been learning a lot in my photography class, and ... well, I think maybe I want to do this instead. Not just as a hobby, but as my career."*

*"Really," I said. "Acting's been important to you for a long time, so I guess this must be pretty serious. Can you say more?"*

*"I'll try," she smiled. "With photography, I'm still being an artist ... but it's more my own work, what I see and choose, not what some other artist writes."*

*"Oh yes," I said. "I get that. It's why I make time to do my own writing."*

*"And then," she added, "you're an actor, and a writer. Em's a writer. Mom does graphic arts, and Timmy, with his drawing and painting ... This is something no one else in the family does. It's just mine."*

*How necessary it's been for Carlie to find her own way — first her place in the family, and then her way of being in the world beyond.*

*I've learned it's natural for a younger child to feel left out. The newcomer has to break into a system everyone else understands and had a place in before she came.*

*But isn't this true for every child? The first one comes naked and defenseless into a world of giants, having to win their attention or die. And must worm a way into that closest of dyads, the mated couple ... making them into parents.*

*And so it is for each, in turn ... Alone in a strange land, lucky if there's a sibling, a small being like yourself who isn't quite so frightening, who might understand ...*

*Carlie's struggle makes me remember what I guess I had to forget as I struggled to fit in, to grow up.*

*I've always loved Wordsworth's image of the child arriving in this world from heaven, trailing clouds of glory ... But childhood's also a terrifying involuntary journey, and the terrors somehow get shoved under the bed ...*

*As a parent, I was so focused on things I could see and deal with — everything from diapers to school uniforms. When I forcibly forgot so much of my childhood's own fearful inner drama, did I blind myself to theirs? I had tried to listen ... but did I hear?*

*Carlie's always been the bold one, the adventurer. I've admired her, loved her for that. But were her risk-taking and courage partly born of desperation?*

*And if so, what can I do about it now?*

*Chapter 6*

## CAVES AND MUD

Something's hitting me in the face, awakening me.

Bark, and bits of twig — they're falling on my face, my chest. I stand up, brush myself off, and see a large red-gold squirrel amid the lower branches, scolding. He turns and with a digging motion throws another shower of duff my way, then faces me, chattering angrily.

"Sorry," I say, laughing. "I didn't know it was your space."

As I walk over to get my shoes, I see a lone sock lying across my pack.

"Hey," I say, looking up. "Not funny."

I sit down to pull on one sock and shoe, and slip the other shoe on my bare foot. I step back, about to address my little antagonist again, when I see the sock — it's lying on a fallen branch about ten feet away, downstream. Before I can ask the squirrel why he did that, the sock moves; it slips over the branch, disappearing on the other side.

I grab my backpack and step carefully toward the branch. The thick mat of needles crunches, and a small figure, several times the size of the squirrel, darts away from the branch where my sock was. It disappears behind a broad-leafed bush.

I'm curious, but I need to cover my foot. So I retrieve the sock and sit on the branch, putting it on. I don't look at the bush; but in a corner of my eye, I see motion. Turning my gaze without moving my head, I see a thin triangular face under the wide green leaves.

Fox.

I can't help smiling. What would a fox want with my socks? The silliness of this unexpected rhyme makes me chuckle aloud, and the little face disappears.

But a moment later, it's back.

"You don't have to hide," I say softly, in the voice I use to calm babies, and birds, and small animals. Sometimes it works. "I'm just waiting here for someone."

This time, it seems to work.

Tentatively, the fox moves out from under the bush, walking close to a tree, then beside another fallen branch, eyeing me. I watch her, moving my eyes to her and away, not holding eye contact.

Then, when she has gone a good eight or ten feet from the bush, she sits. She scratches her belly with a hind leg, then grooms herself, paws over her face and ears, like a cat.

In between strokes, she watches me.

"Hello, sister," I venture. "You are very beautiful."

One delicate paw moves again from her large, feathery ear to her shiny nose. Her bright black eyes watch.

"You are safe. I will not harm you."

She stops stroking and sits. Whiskers out, nose up, she sniffs the air for something.

"Do you know who I'm waiting for?" I ask.

She tips her head, then she rises and walks slowly away from me, downstream, her great silver-tipped tail waving.

I'm about to say goodbye when she stops and turns, regarding me over her shoulder. I chuckle again — it reminds me of Carlie looking back at me on the ridgetop, after peering down into the valley.

My laughing does not seem to bother the fox. But she turns away, walks a few more feet, stops and looks back.

"You?" I ask. "Is it you I'm supposed to meet?"

It's getting on to late afternoon, and I've seen no one else. At least I should learn where the stream goes, I think, and perhaps start looking for a good spot to spend the night.

"Alright," I say, rising, shouldering my pack. "Let's try this."

Fox turns and lopes slowly downstream, every so often stopping and waiting. I stroll along behind, unhurried, wanting to give her room. I wonder, briefly, whether she fears I'm pursuing her; but she keeps trotting along, turning and waiting, not trying to hide or disappear. Which she could certainly do if she needed to.

I laugh again, to think I'm following a fox. Or a fox is leading me. Whatever. Together, we proceed into the forest, along the stream.

After we've gone on quite a while, I see the fold in the

mountains Carlie mentioned. What seemed a solid wall of mountain is actually two ridges that don't meet, but overlap. Our stream flows to the foot of the near ridge, then curves along its base.

We follow the stream around the ridge's end and then around its back, into a shadowed pass. Here, the land begins to drop in gentle steps; now and then, the stream babbles over tiny falls and rapids.

"Do you think maybe there's a place where I can sleep in this pass?" I ask Fox, who is still darting ahead, looking back.

She doesn't reply, but suddenly there comes a sound. It breaks through the quiet of stream and forest, and she slips instantly around a low boulder, behind some ferns.

The sound is a cry, in a voice as large and strong as a human child's. There is pain in it, and fear. I turn toward it.

"I'll be back," I tell Fox. "Someone's hurt."

I push into the underbrush, moving toward the cry. I slip off my pack, thinking I may need to use it like a sling. Then I see a shape moving, about the size of a toddler. As I step around a clump of young aspens, I see it — a baby bear, its soft brown fur splattered with blood, limping and crying.

It turns to me and cries again, raising a gashed forepaw. "Oh, baby," I say softly, "baby, let me —"

I do not say more.

For a tiny instant, I'm aware that although I have stopped, the noise of brush breaking has not. Then something huge and powerful slams into me, a lightning-like pain rakes my leg and back, and I'm spinning, flying, sharp branches tearing at me ...

147

I am awakened in near darkness by something pulling at my shoe. It must be Fox. I'm wrapped in a warm, loud throbbing. I see a shadowy shape like a fern before me. I think I'm hurting, but I can't tell.

"Oh, Fox," I say. "What happened?"

I go to move my arms to sit up — I find pain — I cry out.

"Still," a voice says. "Be still. Don't try to move unless I tell you."

Something pulls on my other foot, turning it, this way, that way, setting it down.

"Can you feel that?"

"Yes," I say. I start to ask where I am, then I recognize the sound of the stream, quite loud, to my left.

"Can you feel that?"

It's a woman, sounds like an old woman. She is lifting and working my left arm.

"Yes."

Then my right arm.

"Yes."

Then my head, lifting, turning right, making me look at roots and dirt. Then left, into her face. It's a small, wrinkled face, with soft brown eyes and neat features, crowned with white hair. She reminds me of my mother's mother. All at once, her eyes cloud and her forehead bunches in worry.

"Have you seen my daughter?" she asks.

"I ... I have seen Fox," I say. Her eyes grow bright, and her face relaxes.

"Blessed be," she says. "You have a deep gash on your leg, but everything seems to work alright. Shall we try sitting up again?"

It is not easy. The throbbing, which seems to come mostly from my leg and back, almost makes me throw up. But with her holding me steady, I'm able to prop up slowly on my elbows, sighing hard.

"Hold," she says.

She turns away. She turns back, and her thin narrow hands are filled with water.

"Drink," she says. She brings three handfuls from the stream, and then reaches into one of several soft cloth bags at her hip. She takes out a strip of bark.

"Chew," she says, thrusting it in my mouth.

At first it's dusty and stiff. Then the bark begins to soften; soon, I taste an oddly pleasant, bitter flavor and the sides of my tongue tingle.

"Don't stop," she says. "I'm going to work on that leg a while. This may burn."

She lifts ribbons of what I at first think is skin away from the inside of my right thigh, and I feel faint. Then I realize it is my torn jeans, wet and heavy with blood. She takes a ball of moss in her right hand and begins to pat it onto my badly cut leg.

I fear each touch will be anguish – instead it's oddly soothing. I relax again, and can make out three long gashes, one very deep.

Then she starts rubbing the thumb and finger of her left hand together and a powder drops out, onto the wounds. I can tell there is a burning, like the flat of a hot knife being laid upon my skin. But in the midst of the throbbing, it is barely noticeable. I exhale again, relieved.

"Keep chewing," she says.

I've stopped without knowing it; I start again, and can barely feel the bark in my mouth. But I'm relaxing from the tightness and fear that gripped my body when I awoke.

She is rinsing the blood out of the ribbons of my torn jeans; then she is lacing some long, soft leaves through them, like weaving. The air seems to be growing lighter —moonlight.

"Welcome, sister," she says. "Thank you for the light. Better late than never," she chuckles.

"Now hold on," she says to me, lifting the weaving she has made in one hand while the other sprinkles more powder in the wound. Then she lays the poultice lightly on it, and binds it with what looks like a flattened, fibrous vine.

"Wonderful," I say, my voice slurring around the bark. "Thank you."

"You've found yourself a good place to sleep tonight," she says. "Rest 'll do you best just now, better than walking. And Bear won't be back."

I reach into my jacket pocket and bring out the scarf Althea has given me.

"Good," she says, and wraps it around my neck, over my throat and chest. "Now lay back and get comfortable."

She disappears, then returns dragging flat, soft cedar branches. She spreads them over me like blankets. Then she leans over and lays her hand on my cheek.

"Chew yourself to sleep," she says. "I'll be back to check on you every now and then."

*Wounded ... pain ... I'd be awash in pain if I weren't so numb ... The warm humming lures me toward the dark of sleep, but I'm afraid to let go, to slip into the water ...*

*As I drift, I feel the memory in my body of another body curling into mine, shaking with quiet sobs ...*

*Carlie, home late from a date, walked into her room after only a muffled "Hi" in response to my sleepy greeting. I got up and leaned over the railing of the loft, calling down toward her bedroom.*

*"Is everything OK, hon?"*

*The door opened, and she peered out.*

*"Can I come up?"*

*She climbed the stairs and sat in my one chair, and I moved to sit on the bed.*

*"How are you?" I began.*

*"Terrible," she said. Her folded hands were trembling. "Dad, I ... I was raped."*

*"Oh, sweetheart," I said. "Are you alright? Shall I take you to —"*

*"I'm okay, Dad. Physically. I knew if I fought I'd just get hurt, so ..." Her words dissolved in tears.*

*I gingerly laid a hand on her shoulder.*

"It wasn't your fault, Carlie." I was having trouble speaking through my own tears. "None of it was your fault. You made a wise decision in a terrible situation."

She nodded. I waited.

After a moment, she sobbed so hard it felt like we'd both die. Then, haltingly, she told as much of the tale as she could. She said she wanted to wait until morning to decide what to do, and just sleep on it.

"Fine," I said.

"Dad," she said, "can I sleep with you tonight?"

"Of course," I said. She went down to take a shower, and I put a second top sheet on the bed.

Alone, waves of rage swept through me — I imagined telling the police, catching the kid and beating him senseless ... But I knew those were just my fantasies, and that anything we actually did had to be her decision. This was her body, her life.

I did some deep breathing, with punches and kicks. Then a few yoga stretches to calm down and get centered. I got back in bed, but couldn't read.

When Carlie came upstairs, her hair wet, she crawled into her sheet holding a stuffed bear and wriggled back until she was snug against me.

I laid my hand on her arm. She yawned, and said a soft "G'night, Dad."

I didn't know if she would be able to sleep, or if I would. I lay there recalling how years ago, each of the four children, in their turn, would appear at our door in the night, with a "sleepy toy" or a pillow in hand, and crawl up into our bed. I was trying to figure out how many years that had gone on, when I heard

*Carlie's breathing change and felt her body shudder, then relax.*

*She was asleep.*

Cold. Cold and stiff.

A low, light mist is rising from the stream, softening the chill of the dawn air.

Sounds — birds and animals and insects, all eagerly awakening — call me back toward consciousness. Morning light pokes at my eyes and I slit them open a bit; ferns, green in the light, hang over me. Light rushes between the delicate fronds, stirring my brain awake.

*I dreamed of Carlie, wounded, on the worst night of her life.*

*Now I'm the one who's wounded.*

*And someone's taking care of me — who? Is she real? A dream? Will she come back?*

I inhale deeply.

The stream's crisp moisture and the earth bank's dark, musty damp pour into my body. They're mixed with the perfumes of opening flowers, and the sweet sharp breaths of cedar, fir and pine that have hung in the air all night. I start to stretch, flexing each muscle carefully before moving. I turn my head, and my neck pops several times quickly, releasing the stress from lying motionless all night.

Stretching pulls in more breath, inviting forest-flavored oxygen into my body and taking the knife edge from several small pains. A big, dull area around my mid-body begins to feel a bit looser, lighter. I rise carefully onto my elbows, fingers of fern tickling my forehead. I lift a hand to brush them away, then open my eyes wide. I see a world — water, light and stones, grasses and trees, shadows, dust motes, transparent winged creatures floating in the light ...

Suddenly, a tiny whirr the size and shape of a thumb appears and hovers just above my knees, gleaming green, with glints of bright red. It leans into a pink blossom, kissing the nectar with its needle beak. I move, and the jeweled being flits away. The creek speaks steadily in my ear.

Even in pain, it is good to be here.

I lift a cedar bough off of me, and try to move to a sitting position. Ponderously, I drag one dull leg up the bank, wincing at shock waves of ache and sudden hot threads of pain.

"Hello. Up early, are we?"

The old woman is stepping quickly along the stream bed toward me, holding a wooden bowl with a cloth over it. Her feet are bare. The skirt of her long yellow-green dress and the fringe of her dark shawl trail behind her lightly.

"This'll get you into the day." She lifts the bowl's cover, releasing curls of steam. "Best drink it off while it's still hot."

The cloudy thick tea, or soup, emits a musky smell like mushrooms. Bits of dark green cling to the sides of the bowl. I drink.

"Thank you again," I manage between gulps. "I don't know what I'd —"

"Not to mind," she says, raising her hand. "All is as all must be. I'll just look at that leg for a minute."

154

She prods gently at the poultice she wove, testing here and there, turning her head as if listening. I note that she does not open it to look at the wound.

"Not ready yet," she smiles. "Of course. But it's cooking nicely."

She takes my ankles and lifts, swinging my legs around so I can bend my knees and sit on the dirt ledge where I have slept.

She takes the bowl and tucks it under her arm.

"Since you're so keen for moving," she says, "Let's see about a walk."


Hobbling along beside the stream, I try not to lean too heavily on her shoulder. But my hurt leg can't take much weight; and her tiny frame is surprisingly resilient, easily carrying as much of myself as I give her.

After a fair distance, the land drops off — the steepest ledge yet. The stream rushes over it, becoming a lively, deep-voiced waterfall. We turn into the forest and reach a natural stairway. Its broad, irregular steps are edged with stones that have earth and grass between them, yet they seem too well-placed to have arrived there by accident.

When our descent is finished, we turn back toward the stream.

Suddenly, we're at the entry of a dwelling cut into the earth bank. In a circle of stones beside the doorway, a banked fire releases thin wisps of smoke. Over it, on a tripod of stout branches, hangs a rude kettle made of bark panels stitched together.

"Here we are," my companion says, leading me to a wide, flat rock littered with needles and soft leaves. She smiles warmly. "A journey well made."

As she helps lower me onto the rock, both of us sigh hard. A cloud crosses her brow.

"Have you seen my daughter?" she asks.

I'm caught off guard, puzzled; the answer this time isn't Fox, something tells me.

"I have seen my daughter," I say.

She purses her lips and looks off, considering this. She turns back to me and smiles.

"Blessed be."

She heads into the little cave, and soon the effort of our walk has me drowsing.

*I've always been the rescuer — and now I'm being rescued.*

*In a single violent blow, the mother bear has made me see, all too clearly, my instinct to reach out and save — before I think. And she has told me a hard truth: The rescuer will be sacrificed.*

*For some reason, I realize, my whole life has been animated by a search-and-rescue mission. The foolish quest of a self-appointed knight, looking for an imprisoned maiden to save.*

*Or perhaps I was appointed by my dad, the one who taught me ...*

*Anyway, since I can remember, I've been drawn as if by some magnetic magic to wounded girls who needed to be noticed, listened to, cared for. They were hidden, but not in towers.*

*My mother carried a hidden, hurt girl. She was allowed to peek out at last in the short stories my mother wrote for her college classes, calling to me as we read them together.*

*My aunt Cindy, her sister, was my first babysitter. Closer in age to me than to her siblings, my mother and uncle. Inside her hid the unwanted baby who'd arrived in the darkest years of the Depression. Cindy, as a young teen, would sneak my brother and me to the forbidden skating rink at the beach. She met boys there, skate-dancing with them — and sometimes secretly kissing them — while we watched, entranced, from the bleacher seats. Then we'd rush to the bus, to get home before my parents ...*

*One day, when Cindy was sixteen, she was gone. Riding to Grandma and Grandpa's house, we were told in hushed tones not to ask, or say her name. A long year later, she was suddenly back, part of the family again. Thin and sad and engaged to be married. And she whispered to us she'd had a baby ...*

*My grandmother treated me as her favorite, her first grandchild. I'd sit in her kitchen early mornings as she made breakfast, and she'd send me to the yard to pick blackberries. When I won an Ivy League scholarship, she gave me my own typewriter. When I flunked out and started over, at the community college near her house, she had breakfast waiting for me each morning. And she was waiting each afternoon to talk over coffee.*

*One day, on her couch, she showed me an old sepia photo of her as a girl. I was shocked to recognize that child, the one whose presence I'd always felt ... Years later, when my grandmother lay dying, that girl looked out through her face to say goodbye ...*

*All my life, these hurt, forgotten girls have called to me. Again and again, I've sought them in friendships, loves, even marriage ... And women who weren't hurting, who hadn't been deeply wounded or who had recovered, seldom drew my attention at all.*

*No surprise that the day my first child was born, as I held that tiny, wounded girl in my arms, she was a perfect "trigger" for my rescue pattern.*

*She set off all my unconscious reactions — committing myself totally, without reservation, to loving her and protecting her, to encouraging her into the world.*

*Not a bad thing for a father to feel about a baby daughter, after all.*

*But by then I'd learned, after much pain, to be wary of that unthinking reflex, that magnetism I was only half conscious of, even as I was being swept away by it.*

I spend three days and nights in the earthen dwelling, eating hot soups and stews, chewing bark strips each night to lull the pain into sleeping. Each night, for three nights, I dream the same dream.

*It is a rainy spring night in New Orleans. I am looking out a high window at a huge old brick building from a century ago. Trees line the sidewalks around it, thick with dark, deep green leaves and bright magenta blossoms. The building is — or was — an orphanage.*

*Through a tall, open window directly across from*

*me, I see a man seated at a table, writing. Down below him, on the sidewalk, almost invisible in the dark and the rain — except when they walk under the feeble gas street lamps — pass two pale, forlorn figures.*

*The man is me.*

*And the two figures, lost in the rain, searching for a home, are my daughters. Emma is leading; her right hand trails behind her, while her left holds a shawl around her head and shoulders.*

*Carlie walks behind, her left hand reaching out to grasp her sister's, her right clutching a single blossom and a wrap that's useless against the rain and cold.*

*They are both crying.*

Each night, I wake up thrashing, trying to cry out, to call my other self to the window, or to call words of comfort to the girls.

Each night, the old woman is ready, handing me hot tea, wiping my forehead. Each day, despite my best intentions, I spend far too much time drowsing and napping. The woman lets me hold things for her as she works, and I help to tend the fire.

The third day, she takes the poultice from my leg to reveal three clean, long scabs forming under it. I'm able to drag a half-dozen sizeable stumps and log-ends to her wood pile. But I feel guilty that I can't be more help.

When we talk, it is about the progress of my healing, or about the task we are doing; or she is telling me bits of forest lore, naming bushes and leaves and flowers and mosses and ferns and fungi, and their countless virtues and uses. I'm amazed at how each thing plays a part in her small, quiet economy.

"You use everything," I say to her, as she is lifting lichen gently from a stone.

"Nothing is ever wasted," she says, winking.

Again and again, I see her careful, intimate way with each plant and bird and animal. I feel comforted by her gratitude toward every creature — and her ability, for all her knowledge of this forest world, to be surprised by it. She often laughs, as lightly as the stream.

On the third day, she ends our afternoon tea with an announcement.

"It is time," she says. "You must leave now. Your leg is strong enough."

She steps into her little house, and emerges wearing a cranberry-colored shawl and carrying a stout, well-carved branch as a walking stick. Its handle glints and shines in her hand; tiny bits of mother-of-pearl are inlaid into it.

"This may help you in uneven places," she says, handing it to me. "That thigh muscle's still hard at work a-building."

We set off, after banking the fire, through the pass, downstream. The land drops several more times, twice in ravines so steep we have to climb down, holding on to roots and vines, to make our way to the next level.

Finally, we arrive on a long, sloping plateau. We can see it widening ahead of us. Late morning, we are out of the forest and the plateau descends in a series of steep, rolling, sun-covered hills.

Almost invisible in the sunlight, a pale sickle of a moon hangs in the sky. To our left, the stream works its way down, staying close to the mountains, which diminish but form an unbroken spine up the middle of the island. Far to our right, the plateau ends in a cliff that plunges to the sea.

We walk along until we reach a stand of huge old cedars, their massive trunks interwoven.

"Here," she says. "Ease that leg a while."

She nods to a cool, cave-like enclosure where the trunks lean together to protect a small hollow. Glad for a respite, I step in. It's larger than it looks from outside, roomy enough for a handful of people to stand. Ferns grow on knobby ledges in the walls; a breeze moves through, and shafts of light pour down, golden with dust, from openings higher up in the joined trunks.

As I'm sitting down gingerly against the curved wall, she reaches out and takes the walking stick.

"I'll use this while you rest," she says.

"Please," I answer.

"My bathing pool is nearby," she says. "Rest. I'll be back when I'm done."

Turning to leave, she looks up into the golden light and sighs; with its glow playing on her face, she reminds me again of my grandmother. She turns back to me, the gold still showering over her.

"Have you seen my daughter?"

This time, an answer comes without thinking.

"I have seen my mother."

"Blessed be," she says, smiling, and then she is gone.

*Mother ... partner ... daughter ...*

161

*What is this thread that winds through and shapes my life? This primal force, as powerful as gravity, that holds my life in its grip, attaching me to mother, girlfriend, wife, daughter?*

*This mysterious bond has twisted and turned, weaving itself into my life. And I suspect it has also been twisted and woven by me — my unwitting needs, my half-conscious acts.*

*If I no longer need to be the rescuer, cannot be — indeed never was — then who am I?*

*And whose girl was I so set on rescuing?*

*Was she mine? Not my daughter, but the girl I couldn't be, didn't dare show, in order to be the man my father wanted? The man my world wanted? Is my long-lost sister, with her red hair, hidden inside me — the maiden imprisoned in the tower?*

*And where am I, who am I, now?*

*Who can I be in relation to the women in my life — including the one, if there is one, inside me? Do I still need a mother's adoring gaze? Am I lost without someone to see me, to listen to my feelings? Do I need to listen to a woman, come to know and love her, to feel that I exist?*

*Must I have another body curled into mine each night so I can make it to morning?*

Footsteps break into my thoughts. Opening my eyes, I see the bright-headed walking stick entering the tree-cave. Carrying it is a woman of perhaps thirty, much taller and straighter than my friend. Chestnut brown hair falls on her shoulders.

Yet she is wearing the cranberry shawl, and what

looks to be the same dress. She looks like my mother did when I was very young.

"Here I am," she says. "Have you rested?"

She holds out both hands, and gives the walking stick to me once I am standing.

"We should be going on."

As we walk down the sloping hills in the midday sunlight, I try to think what to say. But nothing seems worth breaking the silence.

We move at a snail's pace, me halting along on the stick while she holds herself to an easy stroll so as not to leave me behind. Still, in an hour, when the sun has reached the mountaintops and they begin to throw shadows on the plateau, we're perhaps halfway down to sea level.

We stop and rest on a boulder, looking at the panorama below.

"There, at the bottom," she says, "as the hills level out, just where that tall rock stands alone in the sea? See those dark shapes?"

I nod.

"The remains of an old, old village. Just beyond, to the left, do you see there is a break in the mountains?"

Again, I nod, seeing a low saddle in the central ridge.

"The isthmus, the island's narrowest point, is less than a mile wide. Two Moon Harbor lies just on the other side."

She reaches in one of the many folds and pouches of her dress, and offers me a handful of dried fruit and nuts. We eat quietly, enjoying the view and the soft, steady breeze now pouring down off the mountains.

As we rise, she begins talking.

"Old stories name the people who lived in that village the Mud-Faces," she says, smiling, her eyes now more green than brown. "Their village is called Mud Village. Around it, in the hills, are deposits of red and grey clay. The people hunted in these mountains, of course, but they also learned to use the clays, and became gifted pottery makers. They adorned themselves with the clays in their worship, too."

We start walking again; she stays close beside me, talking.

"You have heard about the great war," she says. "Mud Village sent six boats, their warriors painted with clay. Stout Heart, the hunting chieftain, led them. His wife, Star Bride, went into seclusion on the day they left.

"Only two boats returned. Star Bride — who had been waiting, praying faithfully, not leaving their house, for more than two years — was shocked to learn that she had lost both her sons, as well as her only brother.

"The boat bearing Stout Heart also carried two women he had claimed as war prizes. When he announced that he had been sleeping with them and would keep them as wives, Star Bride was desolated.

"For two days, she begged and pleaded and argued, but he would not be dissuaded. On the third day, there was a great ceremony to honor the dead and celebrate the victory. Stout Heart was laying an offering before her on the altar, as he had done after so many hunts, when Star Bride took up the ritual knife and stabbed him to death, screaming."

The young woman touches my shoulder, pointing

toward the ruins, which have grown more distinct as we have drawn nearer.

"That circle," she says, indicating a wide bowl cut into the earth, "is where it happened." I stop to consider this; then we are moving on again.

The couple, she says, still had two younger children. The boy, who showed early skill as a hunter, was named Mountain Walker; his sister, who had a gift for the sacred lore of beekeeping, was called Amber.

"Seeing their mother murder their father," my companion says, "sent both children spinning into madness. They plotted together, and slipped into their mother's bedroom the next night while she slept and killed her — with the same knife she had used to slay their father.

"After the deed," my companion says, "Amber ran to hide in the cave where the bees were kept. But in her wild terror, she upset the hives and they streamed out, chasing her. She then ran to Mountain Walker, and they fled — this way, up the hills into the forest — pursued and tormented by a cloud of bees. They spent a year wandering, living alone in the forest; then they returned to the village.

"According to some stories, Mountain Walker alone was chased by the bees and fled in a boat, to the island where the city of Many Smokes had stood. There, these stories say, a goddess took pity on him and healed him, commanding the bees back into their hives.

"Amber, these same stories say, was nursed in her home, crying and raving, for a year. Then her brother returned and she, too, was healed.

"All the stories agree that eventually, the two young people had to stand together before their people, for murdering their mother. Some say they were stoned to death or sent into exile; others say they were acquitted, after the goddess who had healed Mountain Walker pleaded for them."

We have come to the ruins of the village.

Silently, we walk among the rubble of walls, the midden mounds. We come to the bowl in the earth; it holds the remains of concentric rings of stone seats. No single ring is now fully intact, but many seats are still in place.

"Hold," she says. One hand on my shoulder, she guides me to a seat. "Wait here."

She walks, moving easily over the tumbled stones, until she is far below me, in the center of the bowl, where the ceremonial stage was.

Suddenly, I hear a voice whispering.

"Hold up a hand," it says. I do, startled. On the stage, she waves and laughs, not loud enough to carry to where I am — yet I hear her as easily as if she were beside me. I start to rise.

"Stay," she says in my ear. "There is more I must tell you.

"After a war, a father comes home changed, strange, haunted, not the man the mother married. What if she gradually stops loving him — or still feels love, but can no longer admire or honor him, or desire him?

"Is that a killing?

"What if they have a son, and she fails to hide from him what she is feeling — or not feeling — for his father? Is she murdering the father the boy needs to love, to believe in?"

Her voice quavers, but she goes on.

"What if the mother grows lonely, and her only joy is loving the child? What if little by little, unawares, she draws closer to him than to her own husband. What is this boy to do?"

Her voice is choked now.

"How can he escape this mother, and restore his father to life in his heart? Might he not hate her — kill her? I could not condemn him."

Suddenly, she turns and begins to climb up the other side of the bowl. Trying to rise, I realize I will not be able to run after her. As swiftly as I can, I descend to the stage. Leaning on the stick, I shout:

"Stop! Listen — that is not the whole truth of it!"

I take a breath, then go on in the loudest voice I can manage, the one that flew out of me suddenly one afternoon when a little boy was frightening Emma on the playground.

"My mother gave me life — not only mine, but hers."

My words ring off the stones.

"She never stopped!"

A figure in a cranberry shawl walks out from behind a crumbled building.

"Even when she sought her own life," I say more quietly, "the one she had set aside to be a mother, she shared it. She offered me all she was learning — and anything I needed."

The figure comes closer.

"When we were older," I tell her, letting the stones carry my voice now, "each of us had learned — from our broken marriages — to live more carefully. To be more aware. In that hard time, she worked with me to find a new way to be close, a way that made us both happier.

"And when at last she was dying, she shared that, too. She let me help her leave this world, as she had helped me enter it."

The woman sits.

As she does, a movement catches the corner of my eye. A small figure is peering around the broken base of a column.

"Wait," I say to the woman. I turn to the half-hidden figure.

"Please come out," I say softly. "You are safe."

Slowly, shyly, a child emerges. A girl in a dusty shift, perhaps five or six years old.

"Have you seen my mother?" she asks.

"I have," I say. "She is right here."


When the moon rises out of the mountains, I'm still standing on the stage, leaning on the walking stick, looking back up the long slope where the woman and the girl have disappeared.

A stone clatters behind me.

I turn and see another small figure — this time a young boy, who is climbing down the stone rings toward the stage.

He looks up at me.

"Have you seen my father?"

Vertigo — a loud buzzing in the air, the light fading, then quickly bright. But his face stays in focus, and I still hear his question. I also hear the sea slapping on the shore.

"Yes," I say.

And at once, I know what it is I must do. "I'll take you to him."

I reach out my hand. He takes it, hopeful.

"We have to walk across those hills," I say, pointing to the low saddle in the mountain range. "About a mile, I think. Can you do that?"

He nods, eager. A man on a walking stick with a boy, we set off toward the moon, as fast as we can go.

In about an hour, we have reached Two Moon Harbor. We stop to drink from a fountain, then hurry to the boat docks. The *Mnemos* is there, tied and waiting, where Emma has left it.

"Thank you, sister," I say to her, wherever she is.

When we roll back the canvas cover, the boy hops in. I cast off the bow line, then the stern, and step in after him. Gulls are calling and wheeling.

"I've never been on a sailboat," he says, wide-eyed.

"It's fun," I say, "an adventure. We have a long way to sail. If you get tired, you can sleep on the boat."

His eyes grow even wider. I motion him to sit down as I fire up the little motor. As we're nosing out of the harbor, he goes into the small galley below deck. He comes out dragging a canvas bag.

"What's this?" he asks. I see a note pinned to the bag's drawstring.

*Dear Dad*, it says, *If you've made it this far, you understand why we had to leave. Good sailing.*

Tears cloud my eyes; one drops on the paper.

"It's from my children," I say. "Let's see what's

inside."

He opens the bag and happily pulls out food, water bottles, and blankets. Soon he is sitting, wrapped in a blanket and sucking a cinnamon stick, holding the tiller steady while I hoist the sail.

We're heading into open water.

*Chapter 7*

# DEER ISLAND

We have steady winds, and I keep watching for landmarks. In the fading light of late evening, I see the island with the twin bald mountaintops off to our right; the peaks' western faces gleam with moonlight. We are finding our way.

A gull from Two Moon Harbor has stayed with us, feeling at home in the boat's rigging. From time to time, it rises and circles, scanning for fish, singing out its raucous glee; it always returns, settling with a flap and tuck of its grey-shouldered white wings, and a short laugh from its yellow beak with the one red dot on each side.

The boy, drowsy from excitement, the long walk, and the fresh sea air, rolls up in his blanket on the narrow, cushioned seat. As he drifts to sleep, I watch him.

*I know this face.*

*When he turns slightly, wrinkling his nose at the breeze, I see it. If he were wearing a wide-collared Buster Brown shirt, he could have stepped out of an old photograph I used to pore over — a boy standing beside a pony in Chicago, holding his mother's hand, making a teasing face at the camera.*

*I remember, as a child, puzzling over how my father could have been a child younger than me. Yet I also felt that I knew this boy, had played with him, lived with him.*

*Now, more than forty years later, I begin — at last — to wonder about that feeling. Did I know this boy because he hid behind my father's face, asking to be seen ... to be listened to ... to be cared for?*

Low white clouds scurry over us, hiding the moon as we work westward. Soon, the clouds are many shades of grey, and we're tacking back and forth across the wind that carries them in from the outer ocean.

I see a narrow pass I think Matt and I came through; an orange buoy marks a whirlpool near its mouth. I turn southwest, rounding the buoy, and we're running down the wind, through the pass and into an archipelago of small islands.

Roused by our speed, or perhaps by new scents on the wind, the gull gives a pair of mewing cries and rises up to go scouting.

We continue sailing southwest, working the wind fairly well. I can't pick out the route Matt and I took, but we keep arriving at spots that look familiar, and we make good time. The gull again finds us, and resumes his perch.

"Where are we?"

The boy has awakened, looking up drowsily from his cocoon.

"I think we're less than an hour away," I say. "You were sleeping."

"I was dreaming," he says. "Can I have a drink of water?"

"Sure," I say, shifting the tiller and boom as we leave the lee of an islet. "Everything is for sharing."

He reaches into the canvas bag, takes out one of the water bottles and drinks twice, thirstily. Then he wipes it and hands it to me.

"For sharing," he says.

I smile, taking the bottle from his small hand.

He rummages again in the bag, draws out a loaf of dark bread. He breaks off a chunk, puts it in his mouth, then breaks off another. He crumbles it onto the deck, looking up at the gull. The gull cocks its head; the boy sits back; the bird hops down and grabs the morsels laid out for him.

"What's your name?" the boy asks. I smile at the thought that he's talking to the bird, then see he's looking at me.

"I'm Henry," I say. A look of surprise.

"Me, too!" he shouts.


It takes a little longer than I thought, but soon we come in sight of Deer Island. I recognize the wooded islet on our left, and the long curve of the white beach on our right.

"Here we are," I say. "We'll land on that beach, just a little way down."

Henry hugs the rail, straining to look, hopping with eagerness.

In a few minutes, we're there; I keep up speed, hoping to run the boat well aground, as I'm not sure how far up the beach I can drag it. This makes for a dramatic landing — Henry yelps as we crunch onto the shore, the impact pitching us both forward; the gull shoots out of the rigging in a whir of feathers, calling loudly.

Henry and I manage to tug the boat a bit farther up onto the sand. The gull finds a perch and settles. The two of us walk down the beach, angling toward the woods.

"We're going to do something very special," I tell him as he tugs on my hand, happily kicking the sand. "It may seem a little strange, but it's really important."

He looks up, curious.

"I'm thinking it's what we must do to bring you to your father." Henry gives a smile and looks down, kicking the sand as he walks.

Soon, I see the stone table. When we reach it, we stop. An eagle cries afar off.

"Hop up here," I say, patting the stone's flat top. As Henry scrambles up its rough side, I kneel to look for the small cave-like hole where Dan Paul took out the deerskin bag. I find it and reach in. The bag is there. I pull it out and lay it on the table.

"Here," I say, opening the drawstring to reveal the antler knife. "Pull this out."

Henry slips out the horn knife, fascinated by its

jagged shape, its carved handle.

"Now," I say, "let's hold this."

He wraps his small hands around the tip of the handle, and I grasp it just below them.

"Perfect," I say. "I'm not sure how this'll work, but I've seen something like it before. We probably should close our eyes."

He squints his eyes nearly shut, still watching.

"Now think about a place where you feel safe and happy," I say. "See it in your mind."

We lift the knife slowly, as high as we can.

I see Little Mother lifting her crown up into the sunset.

"Now," I say, "let your heart call out to your father." I fling my soul out in every direction, to any goddesses or gods who are listening.

"From where the moon now stands," I shout, my voice rough and resonant, "We will slay children no more!"

Suddenly, behind us, a voice calls my name — our name. A hand falls on my shoulder.

I turn to see a tall woman, red hair cascading onto wide, square shoulders.

I know her at once. She has walked my dreams since my youth, her green eyes and smile warming my heart.

"Put the knife down," she says. "It is not yours to destroy. Your work is done."

"Done?" I manage.

"Done," she affirms, nodding.

Henry throws his arms around me.

"Dad," he says into my breast.

The woman slips the antler knife into the bag, and puts it away. Turning to us, she lays a hand on my cheek and one on Henry's.

"Time to go," she says. And we walk to the beach.

I can't see the *Mnemos* anywhere.

But ahead of us lies a small wooden dugout canoe, with the squared ends of classic Salish design. She motions us to climb in the front. She gets in back, pushing off, and sets to work with the oar, heading south.

In the darkening night, the rhythm of rowing and the waves' soft talking send me into a drowsy half-dream.

Black against dark, dark blue, silhouettes of land and trees slide by. Towers of smoke rise above them, as if from fires. But they do not wave and curl and wave like smoke.

They are steady.

As I watch, they take the shapes of ancestors and animals, fishes and birds, all hovering in the dark. They seem to be watching us as we pass; mists and rain sometimes slant across them.

A heron calls; then it's a wooden flute, in a long, mournful yet peaceful melody. From where the woman sits and rows, I hear a throaty humming — half her voice, half the cello-like low harp I have heard in my dreams. The music moves gently, steadily, calming and calming.

The next thing I'm aware of is stars against the black deep sky. Then no seeing, just music and water; then silence.

Long, long later, the light returns, calling me into its world.

I have no idea where I am, or when. I sense breathing, hear birdsong. I seem to see a steady, flat geometry of red highlights and deep shadows. Gradually, this settles into a stable form and I recognize beams and planks ... a ceiling.

I am lying down, in a cabin.

The next time I wake, it's early evening.

I sit up. Out a window, the pale, lemon-blue of twilight is filling the sky. One fat star rides the treetops, chasing a huge, unfinished moon. The world is again turning to silhouette.

A small fire crackles in the brick fireplace. A tray sits on the hearth.

I eat, savoring the warmth and the flavors. I'm sipping the strong tea when a knock sounds at the door. A man enters, wearing short-clipped grey hair and a cardigan sweater.

I recognize him: the innkeeper from my first night with Tim.

"Up at last," he says. "Feeling better?"

"Very good, thanks," I say. "And thank you for the food. Where's Henry?"

"Pardon?" he says, brows lifting.

"The boy with me. And the redheaded woman who brought us. Is she still here?"

177

"I think you're still a bit groggy," he says with a smile. "Still in dreamtime. You came alone — last night around midnight."

♦  ♦  ♦

It is three-thirty in the afternoon.

I can see only a slice of sky, misty rain with patches of blue light, transected by steel girders and gigantic window frames. I'm sitting on a bench before Chief and the Family, bathing in the powerful, deep jade calm of their presence.

On my lap lie a pair of photo frames, hinged together. One holds a color picture of my children — Matt, Em, Carrie, Tim — their arms across each other's shoulders. They are relaxed, smiling.

"These," I say silently to the Chief, "are the faces that change." My children, anyone's, Earth's.

"The ones who leave," a deep voice answers from within the mountain of stone.

And I see, with a sharp pang of loss — sharp as the antler knife piercing my chest — that each of my children, after our visit, has left me. As I left them.

I look a long time at the photograph, saying goodbye.

The other frame holds not a photograph, but a print.

It has three colors — red, grey, and black. On a pale grey background, with a wash of darker grey cloud across the top, a dugout canoe slides past the silhouette of a forested island. Lines of thin grey rain slant across everything.

In the center of the canoe sits a man wrapped in a robe, wearing a cone-shaped red hat, staring forward. Before and behind, in their totem masks, sit Fox and Raven, Orca and Eagle — all smiling, rowing.

They draw a small smile from me.

"These," I say, "are the faces that do not change." Each of us, journeying alone into the mist — with the companions we find, or who find us.

I look up at the massive, magnificent statue, into the eyes of Daughter, who wears her braids neatly plaited and gently carries Frog against her breast. Above her, like the sun over a mountain, the face of Chief rises; his shoulders spread on either side of her. I remember Henry, clinging to my chest.

"Oh, Chief," I say quietly. "We cannot do, or we fail to do, so much we wish for them. Is it always so?"

I hear a deep, silent chuckle.

"Always so," says the voice.

I rise slowly to go, feeling a twinge from the scars in my thigh.

"Some," the voice continues, "we do. And that is what matters. Is it not so?"

I stop and turn, and look again at the family.

"It is so," I say aloud.

As I leave for my flight home, I hear voices echoing behind me.

"Blessed be."

# Acknowledgements

My first and oldest debt is to my mother, Eileen Martin, who infused my life with her aesthetic and her commitment to inward exploring; she also provided encouraging support that never wavered. My grandmother, Eva Fink, likewise offered unquestioning love, and a sense that peace could be reached even through the most difficult journey.

My father in journeying, and using language to record it, is Matsuo Basho, who lived and wrote in Japan more than 350 years ago. His *Oku no Hosomichi* (*The Narrow Road to the Interior*) has long been for me the ultimate model of soul story. My "step-fathers" in this work include, of course, Sigmund Freud and Carl Jung, two intrepid explorers and consummate story tellers whose imprint remains vast and legible in our culture.

In midlife, I was fortunate to find and follow a less-taken road, led by the "Dream Tending" work of Steven Aizenstat and the faculty he assembled at Pacifica Graduate Institute. There, I was gifted with such teachers as Marion Woodman, Clarissa Estes, Marija Gimbutas, Thomas Moore, Joseph Campbell -- and Andrew Samuels, who challenged me to look at the central role of fathering in my life. It was also here that I was immersed for the first time in the lore of the ancient Mediterranean peoples.

A clinical internship took me to British Columbia, where I was deeply touched by the art and stories of the Salish and Haida peoples and their reverent tending of their spectacular lands. Here I also met *The Jade Canoe (Spirit of Haida Gwaii)*, the formidable, eloquent statue by Bill Reid that anchors this story and my dream.

My dear friend and collaborator Karen Moran accompanied me through early attempts to write about fathers and their children, especially daughters. She also listened, read, and gave feedback through more than 20 years of drafts and reworkings that have become *Father Dream*.

I must thank Vicky Gardner for lending me a home and giving my first draft an enthusiastic reading, and Kathleen Parry for midwifing the final draft from hyperspace to print, complete with her exciting cover design.

Finally, I thank each of you who reads this. May this story lead you into your own dream, and help you create the story of "your one wild and precious life."

## About the Author

MARK HEIN is a divorced father of four adult children. After a career as a journalist, he studied psychology and myth, focusing his studies on the myths of native cultures, while training as a psychotherapist. Now mostly retired, he works as a writer and artist from his home in the mountains of Los Angeles.

Made in the USA
Middletown, DE
28 October 2022

13690401R00102